FIGHT FOR LOVE

DELANEY DIAMOND

GARDEN AVENUE PRESS

Fight for Love by Delaney Diamond

Copyright © 2011, Delaney Diamond

Garden Avenue Press

Atlanta, GA

ISBN: 978-0-9852838-8-9 (Ebook edition)

ISBN: 978-1-940636-50-4 (Paperback edition)

CHAPTER 1

*R*ebekah Jamison wiped sweat from her cheeks with the back of her forearm so she wouldn't scratch her face with the rough, dirty gloves she wore. The edges of her headscarf were damp. The cut-off denim shorts and loose-fitting tank top had seen better days, but they were comfortable, and she preferred to wear as little clothing as possible when she worked in the yard. The vegetable garden was a treat, but it could also be quite taxing in the Georgia heat.

"Mom, look!" her eight-year-old called from a few feet away. He was grinning broadly, holding a worm in his palm for her to see.

"Sweetie, put that down," Rebekah scolded from her position on her knees.

She had encouraged him to help her plant the fall vegetables, but he was turning out to be a distraction she didn't need. Every so often he would wander away from the task, digging in the dirt where she didn't tell him to dig and chasing after wasps and butterflies that flitted around the small, privacy-fenced yard.

She probably would have been farther along if he weren't "working" with her, but she enjoyed their moments together.

Nine months out of the year she taught middle school kids about conservation, alternative energy, and green living as a science teacher in metro Atlanta. The biggest perk of working for the school system was that she could spend the summers with the favorite man in her life.

Rebekah rose to her feet and dusted off her knee pads. "Maybe it's time for a break," she announced. She removed the large straw hat providing protection from the scorching sun.

"Can I have some sweet tea?" His brown face looked up at her expectantly. He was overdue for a haircut. The loose, dark curls on his head were thick and unruly. With his cute, angelic face and big gray eyes staring up at her, she couldn't refuse him the indulgence this time.

"Yes, but only if you drink a glass of water right after."

"I will, I will," Ricardo promised, racing past her toward the back door of the kitchen.

She would make sure he drank water the rest of the day. He had developed a sweet tooth of late, and she wanted to break him from the habit of sugary drinks. Besides, he needed to stay hydrated since he spent so much time outdoors.

Rebekah removed her knee pads and gloves and circled the small area where this year's crop of summer vegetables was planted. She smiled. Last year she'd had enough squash, tomatoes, cucumbers, and green peppers to share with her parents and a couple of neighbors. This year's crop appeared just as healthy and bountiful.

The ringing of the doorbell brought her head up.

"I got it!"

"Ricky, don't open the door unless you know who it is first."

He knew better, but it didn't hurt to remind him. She hoped it was the delivery she was expecting from her sister, Samirah. They were souvenirs for the family from her latest jaunt overseas. She often sent them nice gifts from her travels. Rebekah sometimes envied her younger sister's carefree lifestyle.

Samirah had a culinary degree from Le Cordon Bleu, and she traveled the world, earning her keep as a cook in restaurants or private residences.

"Mom, come quick!"

Rebekah dropped everything in her hands and raced into the kitchen, uncertain if Ricardo's tone expressed excitement or anxiety.

He stood in front of the open front door, staring at someone outside. As she came closer, he caught sight of her and began to hop up and down excitedly, pointing with his hand to the still-invisible person on the other side of the threshold.

"Look! Look! It's *La Sombra*, Mom! It's *La Sombra*!" he screamed excitedly.

Rebekah skidded to a halt, her feet no longer sure what to do since her brain temporarily ceased to function. Heavy knots piled up in her stomach, and her broken breath shivered past her suddenly parched lips.

It couldn't be him.

Ricardo's face was alight with glee, and his uncontrolled excitement was a comical contrast to the heavy dread pressing down on her. She moved slowly toward the door, closing her hands into tight fists to calm their shaking.

When the person came into view, her stomach muscles clenched into even tighter, more painful knots.

There was no doubt who the man was at the door. It had been nine years since she'd last seen him in person, but his image appeared on the occasional magazine, and she'd read articles about him online. Even if he weren't a public figure and she had wanted to forget him, it would have been impossible because of the pint-sized, darker version of him bouncing up and down like a rubber ball just a few feet away.

La Sombra had been the alias he used when he was a professional wrestler. The nickname, which meant "the Shadow" in Spanish, had stuck because of his dark complexion. His real name was Rafael Lopez, and he was her ex-husband.

His gaze lifted from the small boy before him and settled on her. From the firming of his sculpted mouth and the hard glint that came into his gray eyes, she knew he'd already deduced the obvious.

The young boy whose excited reception he had just received was the son he had never known existed.

CHAPTER 2

*R*ebekah placed her hand on Ricardo's shoulder. "Ricky, go upstairs, sweetie," she said. "I need to have a word with…" She didn't even know what to call him "…with Mr. Sombra."

"But Mom…"

She gave him her stern face that meant she wasn't playing around. *"Now."*

With a heavy pout, Ricardo stomped toward the staircase.

"Ricardo Lopez," Rebekah said, "do you want me to follow you and give you something to stomp about?"

He froze with his hand on the wooden stair rail and peered over his shoulder at Rebekah with a hurt expression on his face. "Sorry, Mom," he said quietly. Twisting his head further without turning completely around, he looked at Rafael, who hadn't made a move during the short tantrum. "Please excuse my behavior, Mr. Sombra. My mother raised me better than that."

Rebekah almost smiled as he repeated almost verbatim words she'd said to him on other occasions. His pitiful expression almost undid her, but she kept her face in an unhappy scowl.

"Will I be able to get his autograph?" her son asked.

"Yes," Rafael interjected. He stepped into the house, and the expansive width of his broad frame blocked most of the outdoor light. "Just as soon as your mother and I have a little chat."

Ricardo's face broke out into a happy grin, and he scampered up the stairs.

Rebekah's heart kick-started with a thump, the matter-of-fact tone doing nothing to allay the frisson of fear that trickled down her spine. Even more disconcerting was her reaction to the deep, seductive sound of his accented voice. It scrambled her brain and sent unwelcome vibrations running through her.

She didn't dare look at him, worried he'd see every emotion she felt. Shame. Excitement. Anxiety. She needed time to gather her thoughts so she could have a coherent conversation. The shock of his unannounced arrival sharply tipped the balance of her normally ordered day toward disorder.

Deafening silence descended between them, and Rafael was the first to break it. "We need to talk."

As he shut the door on the outside world, Rebekah finally ventured a look at him. His thick black hair was closely shorn to his head. At five-feet-seven, she wasn't a small woman, but Rafael dwarfed her at six-foot-three. He had an incredible physique, with muscles so densely packed the linen button-down shirt couldn't conceal them. His muscles were tightly honed from years of weight lifting and hours of exercise, creating a fighting machine of flesh-covered steel. Each meaty bicep was the size of one of her thighs, and his lean fingers looked long enough to span the width of a basketball.

"Sexiest Athlete Alive," headlines had proclaimed two years in a row. More recently, his rugged good looks could be seen smiling into the camera endorsing agave nectar, an all-natural sweetener exported from Mexico.

When his dark gaze rested on her, the last remnants of

rational thought disappeared like a puff of smoke in a blast of wind. For a few seconds, her breath caught in her chest, and she was once again the seventeen-year-old girl who had anxiously awaited her eighteenth birthday so she could run away and marry the man of her dreams. He became the twenty-year-old rough neck from south of the border who had captured her heart and convinced her not to judge a book by its cover. His coarse exterior had disguised a tender heart and loving disposition—or so she'd thought. Her disapproving parents had been correct in their initial assessment of him. Rafael had changed once they were married, and not for the better.

"What are you doing here?" Rebekah asked.

The cold stare of his eyes lanced through her. "Is that any way to greet a man you haven't seen in almost ten years?"

Of course not. If her beating heart had anything to say about it, he would have received a much warmer greeting. "You came here unannounced, uninvited to my house. Something tells me this isn't a social call."

"I came because I had something I needed to tell you—in person," he said. "I didn't want to tell you over the phone. I'm on my way to New York and decided to stop over in Atlanta to see you."

"You could've called first, instead of popping up unannounced. As you pointed out, it has been almost ten years."

His lips thinned in irritation. "For the record, once I tracked you down, I did call, but you don't have voicemail, so I couldn't leave a message. Since I couldn't get in touch with you, I figured it was easier to show up."

Rebekah could have kicked herself. She had ordered the VOIP phone service over a week ago, but since she was a technophobe, she had delayed setting up the voicemail.

"I have caller I.D. I never saw—"

"My number is private. You wouldn't *see* anything."

Rebekah swallowed. Since he'd seen Ricardo, she could

understand his antagonism, but she had reasons of her own to feel antagonistic toward him. "What's so important you had to tell me in person?"

"Are we going to have this conversation in the middle of your foyer? Is your southern hospitality only reserved for people you're expecting?"

Without waiting for a response, he brushed past her toward the kitchen, and she caught a whiff of an unfamiliar cologne. She followed him on unsteady legs, conscious of the fact she looked as bad as he did good. While he was dressed comfortably in a fine linen shirt and crisply pressed dark slacks, she was self-conscious about her unattractive gardening attire and pink cotton headscarf. She wasn't wearing a stitch of makeup, and she was certain she must smell sweaty after working in the yard.

In the kitchen, Rafael leaned against the counter, staring at her as she leaned against the counter across the room. His arms hung loosely at his sides, but she could sense the leashed tension in him.

"Well?" she said to break the uneasy silence.

She was never good at remaining quiet, and he was the complete opposite. He was the quintessential strong, silent type.

"Is he mine?"

She hadn't expected him to ask that question first, but it was inevitable. "Yes."

Rafael's hands clenched into fists, and he pushed away from the counter and took two long strides toward her. Rebekah brought her hands up in a defensive motion, drawing in a sharp breath. His steps came to an abrupt halt.

"I wasn't going to hit you," he rasped.

"You're not exactly known for your long fuse." Her rapid heartbeat began to slow down.

"I would never hit a woman, no matter how much she infuriates me." His cold, angry eyes stared into hers. "How could you do that?" he demanded in a rough voice. "How could you keep him a secret from me?"

Now came the hard part—the inadequate explanation she couldn't even justify to herself. "I did try to contact you, but you were always traveling. It was impossible to get in touch with you."

"You didn't try hard enough." He found her guilty and delivered a cutting indictment. His eyes were filled with accusation. He swiveled on his heel and stalked over to the door. He stared out the window at the backyard, his shoulders rigid and his neck muscles taut. "*Dios*, Rebekah, how could you not tell me?"

The beseeching sound of his voice tore at her conscience. There was nothing she could say to make what she had done acceptable. She *had* tried to contact him, but he was right. She hadn't tried hard enough. They were separated and on their way to divorce when she'd found out about her pregnancy.

She had been back in Atlanta at her parents' house, and he had already moved to California with Marty Luger. Marty had managed Rafael's career from the time he discovered him at a local fight club in Las Vegas. They had moved there after she graduated from high school, and they got married in a small chapel off the strip.

At first, it seemed the best decision was to remain quiet. His life on the road had concerned her, and his career was taking off. With her youthful dreams crushed under reality's ruthless boot, she had felt like an extra appendage. She was certain the last thing he wanted was to be saddled with a child, and she certainly hadn't wanted him to think she was using their son to make claims on his impending fortune.

"I was protecting him."

"From his own father?" Rafael grated.

"Yes! I didn't want him exposed to your lifestyle—the drugs, the women, the drinking, and the brutality of that thing you call a sport."

"It doesn't excuse what you did." His eyes lowered to her belly. "You robbed me of the chance of watching your body swell with my child and robbed me of the first years of his life."

His bitter words were like lashes across her conscience. "I was nineteen. I didn't know what to do at the time. It was the wrong decision, I know, but I did what I thought was best."

"Is that all you can come up with?"

"It's the truth, Rafe."

His gaze swept her face. "What about later? What about when you turned twenty-one? Or twenty-two? Or even now, at twenty-eight? When exactly did you decide it was the wrong decision? When I walked through the door just now and saw him standing there, looking so much like me it's a wonder he didn't figure it out himself?"

"Fine!" She pushed away from the counter to face him squarely, trying to quell the trembling in her stomach. "What I did was wrong. But let's get one thing straight, if you had been the husband you were supposed to be—if you hadn't done what you did—I wouldn't have hesitated to tell you about Ricardo, and you would have been by my side the entire time, instead of out in California"—she waved her hand in a sweeping gesture—"sleeping with every woman who tossed a smile your way."

Sickening thoughts of him with other women raced through her mind. How many had warmed his bed over the years? Had they willingly done the things she wouldn't?

His face hardened and angry color tinged the light caramel of his cheeks. "It didn't take you long to bring that up. You couldn't wait to throw it in my face, could you?"

Rebekah knew her comment was a low blow, but she couldn't stop herself. Before the flash of anger, she saw the hurt in his eyes. She pushed aside the pang of guilt. She was right to feel angry, and she wouldn't feel guilty about it.

"You know what you did." The painful burning in her throat indicated the hurt from his betrayal hadn't disappeared. It had only lain dormant, and seeing him again brought it back to life —almost as fresh and new as the day he'd broken her heart and rendered their marriage vows void and useless.

"Yes, I know what I did," he agreed tersely, "and now I know what you did."

The air was thick with the animosity that flared between them. Rebekah took a deep, shaky breath. "Throwing accusations around isn't going to get us anywhere."

"No, it isn't," Rafael conceded. He eyed her with a frown. "We need to decide what we're going to do about Ricardo."

Her ears perked up. "What do you mean 'what we're going to do about Ricardo?'"

"What do you think I mean? He's mine."

"He isn't a possession, Rafe, like one of your fancy cars or your championship belt. He's a person."

His dark eyes flashed angrily down at her. "You think I don't know that? But he is *my son*, and I intend to be a part of his life from now on. First, we need to tell him right away that I'm his father. Then, I want him to come spend time with me in California. I have no idea what he believes, but you'll make sure he understands I *did not* desert him all these years."

His dictatorial tone rubbed Rebekah the wrong way, but she bit back her angry retort. Under the circumstances, it would be an overreaction, but she wasn't far from giving him a piece of her mind.

"All right," she said. "I'll have a talk with him later."

A muscle in his jaw tightened. "You'll have a talk with him now, while I'm here. You're no longer a single parent. We'll do this together. "

"Do you have to talk to me like that?" she snapped.

"Only if you fight me on this. Is that what you intend to do?"

"No. Of course not. I'm worried about how this will affect him. We're about to dump a lot on a kid who, for eight years, has never had a father. Now, all of a sudden, here you are, bigger than life. I don't even know how he knows who you are. You retired almost two years ago, and I certainly never allowed him to watch wrestling."

It was possible Ricardo had seen the replayed matches on television without her permission. It could even be from the occasional commercials Rafael shot. Since retiring from wrestling, he endorsed a variety of products. In addition, he'd licensed his name on a chain of gyms on the west coast.

"He's a boy," Rafael said. "When I was his age, I was curious about fighting. He could have found out about me—my persona —from one of his friends at school. It's natural for boys to be into that kind of thing."

Rebekah knew he was right, but she had no interest in fighting and tried to limit her young son's exposure to violence. The idea of co-parenting with Rafael was daunting, and she had no idea what kind of parent he would be. He deserved the opportunity to play that role, but she'd had Ricardo to herself for eight years. She would have to relinquish any hard feelings she harbored toward Rafael and allow him to participate in all aspects of his son's life. Her only fear was that their parenting styles would be so different he would undo everything she'd taught their son.

"About California," she began, "what did you have in mind?"

"He could come spend the summer with me in L.A."

"I don't know, Rafe. The entire summer is a bit much. Let's take it one step at a time, okay? We'll see how he handles finding out you're his father, and then we'll go from there."

"Rebekah, I'm asking for one summer." The underlying accusation being she had robbed him of eight years.

A tug of war for Ricardo's time had already begun. He didn't even consider they may already have plans. "I understand, but I was thinking about taking him to St. Kitts to see relatives this summer. I think it would be better if we put off this conversation until later."

St. Kitts was a small island nation in the Caribbean where her mother was from. As children, she, Samirah, and their older brother, Adam, spent their summers there. As the years passed, they visited less frequently, but she wanted her son to be aware of his Caribbean roots. The last time he visited was at the age of five, and he hardly remembered his time there.

"All right," Rafael agreed. Rebekah eyed him suspiciously. That was almost too easy. "Are you ready?"

Nodding, Rebekah resigned herself to what was to take place. There was no point in a delay. That didn't keep the bundle of knots in her stomach from reappearing, and she wondered how she would make it through the difficult explanation without looking like a villain.

As they neared the staircase, she turned to Rafael. "Wasn't there something you said you needed to tell me?" she asked.

Rafael looked intently at her, as if trying to gauge how to say what he was holding. "As a matter of fact, there is."

"Well, what is it?"

"I came here to tell you when we signed the divorce papers nine years ago, there was a problem at the courthouse. Our papers were never filed. Legally, you're still my wife."

CHAPTER 3

*R*afael could relate to the stunned look on Rebekah's face. Her expressive, cocoa-colored eyes held a look of such bewilderment, he was certain she would collapse at any moment. No doubt he'd had a similar expression when his attorney had informed him of the error.

She reached wildly for the wooden handrail of the staircase for support. He grasped onto her instead, holding her steady just above her elbow. The softness of her skin sent shock waves through him.

"Take a seat," he said firmly, escorting her to the carpeted stairs where she collapsed with a thump.

He needed a seat, too. The simple act of touching her arm had caused his heart rate to accelerate way too fast. His body recognized hers right away. When he released her, his fingertips still burned with the memory.

She had gained weight over the years, but it had settled in all the right places. Her hips were rounder and more pronounced. Her waist, though not as small as before, was still spannable with his two hands.

Her breasts were definitely fuller. He struggled not to stare at them in the little pink tank top. She wasn't wearing a bra, and her large nipples protruded against the thin material. She hated the size of her nipples, but he'd always loved them, and how sensitive they were. The sound of her moans as he sucked them and stroked them with the tip of his tongue had been music to his ears. He would kill to pull one into his mouth right now.

"Tell me this is some kind of sick joke," she whispered, looking up at him as if she really expected him to take back what he'd said.

She wasn't wearing any makeup, allowing her natural beauty to shine through. Rafael swallowed. He could tell she had been working in the yard. The muskiness of her feminine scent wafted up into his nostrils. He turned his back on her, trying hard to maintain his composure and erase the underlying smell of a familiar tropical fragrance that lingered to tantalize his senses.

"I wish I could," he said. When he felt strong enough, he faced her once more. "My attorney explained it to me. Nine years ago, the clerk responsible for our case accidentally clipped it to the back of another case, so it was never signed by the judge. The misfiling was discovered a couple of years later during an audit, but they were never able to find either of us. Since we never responded to the notices, our case was dismissed."

She stared up at him, eyes still opened wide in shock. Both her upper and lower lashes were long and curled, forming a frame around almond-shaped eyes whose beauty had snared him from the first day they met.

The jolt of seeing his son had somewhat worn off. Now all his senses were concentrated on the woman before him—the woman neither his mind nor his body had been able to forget. The woman who, despite his best efforts, he couldn't stop imagining beneath him, writhing and moaning with pleasure.

"What if one of us had gotten remarried?" Rebekah asked.

The possibility she might have remarried had crossed his mind when he had looked for her. The fact that she mentioned such a scenario had him wondering if there was a promising prospect.

"That would have been a problem, of course." His voice sounded fittingly casual. "Dating will be out of the question until we can get this straightened out."

If it were anyone else, he knew they wouldn't care—not when nine years had already passed. But he knew Rebekah's staunch moral code, and he couldn't resist dropping that little nugget into the conversation. If she was dating anyone seriously, there was no way she would continue the relationship now that she knew they were still married.

A shadow crept into her eyes, darkening the vivid pools of dark brown to almost black. Without saying a word, she let him know there was someone, and the thought dealt a devastating blow to his midsection, more powerful than any fist he'd encountered inside or outside of the ring.

"I suppose you're right," she murmured, averting her eyes. Her shoulders drooped almost imperceptibly. The enormity of his visit, his discovery of his son, and their still intact marriage seemed to weigh her down.

"It was a shock to me, too. I've spoken to my attorney about how to proceed. Of course, that was before I knew about Ricardo."

Her eyes flew to his face. By her expression, she already knew what he was about to say. The pulse at the base of her throat started to beat rapidly. "Custody." Her words were laden with dread.

He nodded.

There was no point in beating around the bush. He had a son, and he intended to be an integral part of his life from now on. He also needed to provide for his care. He glanced around the small foyer. The modest house with its simple furnishings was adequate, but he could provide a lot more, and he intended to. He wanted his son to have all the things he hadn't as a boy growing up poor in Mexico City.

"What do you intend to do?" Her expression was guarded, and she eyed him as if he were a predator trying to breach her defenses.

"I'm not trying to take him away from you, but I want my fair share of time. I've lost a lot of time already. Joint custody with us alternating holidays, maybe him spending summers with me out in California. I'm not asking for everything, but you have to give me something."

Rebekah flew to her feet. She looked him right in the eye. "How long do you intend to play Daddy?"

He was taken aback by the question. "What the hell is that supposed to mean?"

"How long, Rafe?" she asked again. "I won't let you get his hopes up, hurt him, like..."

"Like what, Rebekah?" he demanded harshly, already knowing the answer, bracing himself for her verbal blow.

"Like you did to me!" She averted her eyes, swallowed, and then raised her gaze to his again. He could see the remnant of pain in the depths of her dark brown eyes. Knowing his actions caused it made him clench his jaw so tightly his teeth ached.

"You got tired of playing husband," she continued in a quieter voice.

"So that's the real reason you kept him from me," Rafael said, as if he had just solved a riddle. She frowned in confusion. "To punish me for what I did, you kept Ricardo a secret all these years."

Rebekah's eyes widened in disbelief. "You can't really think—"

"Why not?"

"Because it doesn't make any sense! If I wanted to hurt

17

you, I would've made sure you knew about your son and I would have made sure you had as little access to him as possible."

"No, this way, it's better. You were quietly biding your time until the day you would tell me and I couldn't do anything but accept the fact I had lost all those years."

"This is ridiculous," Rebekah said in exasperation. "I'm not that conniving. You've obviously been jaded by the lack of character in the sluts who fawn all over you in Hollywood."

He stepped angrily toward her, but this time, she didn't retreat. She stood her ground, almost eye to eye with him on the bottom stair. The only indication she was even the least bit disturbed was in the almost unnoticeable tightening of her hand on the balustrade.

"You always could make my blood boil," he ground out. In more ways than one.

He lowered his gaze to take in the rise and fall of her breasts beneath the pink top. The provocative protrusion of her nipples against the material tortured him mercilessly. The shallow inhalation of her soft breaths teased his senses and stoked the flame of arousal in his loins.

He could clearly see in her face that she was not any more immune to him than he was to her. Without thinking, he reached up to stroke her face, and was rewarded when her hand swatted his away.

"Don't you dare touch me," she whispered fiercely, her eyes darkening in anger. Had he imagined the desire he saw smoldering there? "Don't think for one minute that because of an unfortunate twist of fate that kept us married you have any right to touch me. You gave up that right years ago."

"I suppose you've had plenty of opportunity for exploration since then." He shouldn't have mentioned it, but he couldn't help himself. His stomach muscles tensed as if in preparation for a punch.

"I suppose it's none of your business," Rebekah replied with a defiant tilt to her chin.

The irony of the situation wasn't lost on him. Over the years, he'd used other women to help him get over losing her, yet here he was, torn apart by jealousy at the thought that any other man had touched what was his.

Rebekah took a deep breath. "Let's get this over with." She marched up the stairs.

Rafael followed more slowly. He took in the view from a few feet behind her, the curve of her bottom and the shapely brown thighs in a pair of cut-off denim shorts. Thighs he wished he could now slide between and ease this voracious craving for her.

Emblazoned in his mind was the image of her beneath him in their bed, his fingers entwined in the tangled disarray of her long hair as she moaned her encouragement. He could still hear the sweet words. *Mmm...yes, I like that...please...don't stop...ahh... Rafe...Yes! Yes!*

He had been her first. Every chauvinistic bone in his body rebelled against the thought that others had been in her bed and now knew the truth beneath her reserved exterior—that she was a passionate, giving lover. That even though he had prided himself on being her teacher, the exuberance of her responses and sweetness of her touch had wielded substantial power over him. More than she even realized.

THEY SAT on either side of Ricardo on his bed and explained Rafael was his father. The conversation went better than expected.

After his apparent confusion at the turn of events had worn off, Ricardo was almost giddy with joy. He wanted to call his best friends and tell them, who Rebekah found out were the ones who had introduced him to Rafael's past as *La Sombra*. One of the boys was a couple of years older than Ricardo, and he was the one who had shared Rafael's wrestling persona with him.

Then he wanted to know if Rafael could come to school with him in the fall, so he could show him off to his entire class. Overall, he took it very well.

When he asked why his father hadn't come to see him before, Rafael took charge of the answer. Without really explaining, he told Ricardo that would change and he would be in his life from now on.

"What should I call you?"

"What do you want to call me?" Rafael countered. His jaw became rigid with tension.

Ricardo dipped his head shyly. "Can I call you Dad?"

Rafael swallowed, and then he ran his hand over his son's curls. "I would love it if you called me Dad," he whispered in a thick voice.

Rebekah turned away briefly, tears momentarily clouding her vision.

"Are you moving here?" Ricardo asked.

Rafael shook his head. "No, I won't be. I live in California."

"Can I come visit?"

"Of course you can," Rafael replied. His eyes found hers over the top of Ricardo's head. "I was just talking to your mother about a visit to California."

Ricardo's head swung toward her, and Rebekah summoned a smile, hoping it appeared more genuine than it felt. "That's true, Ricky. Your father and I were just talking about that. Maybe you could spend some time with him later this summer."

"Cool!" His eyes lit up. "Do you live on a beach?"

"Not on a beach, but near it."

"Yes!" Ricardo pumped his fist. "Last summer, we went to visit Uncle Adam in Miami, and me and Mom built a sand castle. We can do that again, Mom. It'll be fun!"

"Ricardo, your mom won't be coming. It will just be you and me, so we can get to know each other."

Ricardo's enthusiasm took a nosedive. He leaned closer to his mother, resting his small hand on her thigh. "I don't wanna go without my mom," he said in a small voice.

"Sweetie, it's okay. You should spend some time with your dad. It'll be difficult for me to leave everything behind here."

His pitiful eyes pulled at her heart. "But you don't work in the summer, Mom. You can come with us." He turned to face his father. "Can my mom come?"

Rafael's eyes found hers again. "Yes, your mom is welcome to come, if she would like."

They both turned to Rebekah to get her answer. Her mouth fell open, but nothing came out. Flying to California to spend time in Rafael's company was a disturbing thought, but how could she back out of it when Ricardo so clearly wanted her there? And if she did say no, it would affect her son's decision to take the trip with his father.

She smiled down at her son. "I'd love to come," she said.

"Good." Rafael rose from the bed. "So you'll both spend the rest of the summer with me."

"Wait a minute…"

"Yeah!" Ricardo shouted.

"…the whole summer is a bit much."

The entire situation had gotten out of control. There was no way she could spend the entire summer in Rafael's company. There was still a twinge of attraction there, despite her rapid-fire reaction earlier to dispel any such thought in his mind. Besides, what would she do out in California for the next seven and a half weeks?

"It'll be fun, like Ricardo said." Rafael looked rather pleased with himself. He'd gotten his wish after all. "I'll show you both around L.A., and we can build sand castles every day."

"Yeah!"

If she could have shot daggers at him with her eyes, she would have. "I have things to do here in Atlanta."

"But you're on summer break," Ricardo reminded her helpfully. He was always helpful at the wrong times. Why couldn't he have provided this kind of unasked assistance when she was working in the garden earlier?

"I volunteer at a local women's charity called Second Chance Closet every summer. They need me." Her reason was weak, but surely there was some way out of spending the entire summer with her ex—no, estranged—husband?

"I'm sure they can find someone else to help them this time," Rafael said calmly.

He opened his mouth to say something else when Ricardo sprang to his feet and started doing a little dance. Head and knees bent, hands in the air, he wiggled his body to his own silent beat. A bewildered expression came over Rafael's face, and Rebekah covered her mouth to stop from laughing.

"That's his happy dance," she explained. "He does it whenever he's very excited about something."

"Oh."

Their gazes met and they smiled at each other over his head. It was the first time she'd seen a smile since his arrival. It revealed the twin dimples, one slashed into each cheek. In that brief moment, there was a connection, and her heart did an odd little flip-flop.

Not good.

CHAPTER 4

*R*afael left soon after the conversation with Ricardo. Before his departure, he informed Rebekah he would be in New York for the next couple of days. On his way back, he would stop by so they could make plans to leave for California and decide how to proceed with the divorce.

She made a mental note to contact Buchanan, Rothstein, and Hoyt to set an appointment for a consultation on Friday. Sterling Buchanan, one of her brother's best friends, was a respected attorney with a young, energetic firm in Atlanta. She trusted him to give her good advice.

Rebekah finished up in the garden while Ricardo went across the street to the neighbor's house to share his exciting news with his friends. It was just as well. He couldn't make it any more obvious he had no interest in mucking about in the dirt unless it was under his terms.

Tomorrow was the weekly Thursday night dinner with her parents. She would wait until then to tell them in person that not only was Rafael back in her life, but she was still married to him. She had a pretty good idea how they would react—especially her father. She could only imagine what the dinner conversation would be like as he issued warnings to her, while also trying to refrain from badmouthing Rafael in the presence of his grandson.

She focused on the task at hand, not allowing the incredible truth that she and Rafael were still married to distract her from her gardening.

That night, Rebekah sat in bed in one of her nightshirts. A pillow protected her bare legs from the warmth of the laptop resting on her outstretched legs. She was checking her email when she heard the door click open.

"Mom?"

Ricardo's little round face poked into the room.

"What's wrong? Can't sleep?" Without responding, he came all the way in and stood beside her bed. "What's wrong, sweetie?"

"Do you think my dad will come back?" he asked quietly.

"Of course he will. Why would you ask that?" Rebekah placed the pillow and laptop into the middle of the bed to give him her undivided attention.

Ricardo shrugged, turning his eyes downward.

"Ricky, why did you ask me that?" She swung her legs over the side of the bed.

Ricardo looked up at her again, his gray eyes wide in his face. "I never met him before because he was gone a long time. I want him to come back. I don't want to do anything to upset him."

As if the guilt couldn't get any worse.

Rebekah clasped her son's face in both her hands. "Your father loves you, and there is nothing you could do to upset him so that he won't come back. The reason he wasn't around before was because—well, sometimes grownups do stupid things, and me and your father did something stupid when we were younger, and that's why he wasn't able to see you before. But it had *absolutely* nothing to do with you. Understood?"

He nodded, pulling his bottom lip between his teeth.

"He told you he would take you to California, didn't he?" Ricardo nodded. "Well, then, that's what he'll do. Okay?"

"Okay." A slow smile brightened his face.

Rebekah took him back to his room and made sure he was settled before she returned to hers. She didn't doubt Rafael would keep his promise, but she already knew what she would do if he didn't. She would hunt him down and put her hands around his thick neck and strangle him. She would not let him break any promises to their son the way he had with her.

She found it difficult to concentrate on responding to her email messages. Her vision became obscured with memories.

Her parents had never approved of Rafael. He was too rough around the edges. It didn't help she was still in high school, with a curfew. He worked at a local auto parts store, which was where they had met. She had gone in to get new windshield wipers for the car she had been gifted with from her parents her senior year. Rafael had come out to the parking lot to help her install them.

The attraction had been instantaneous. It wasn't just that he was good-looking. He had made her laugh, too, so by the time he asked for her phone number, she had been completely at ease with him and didn't think twice about giving it to him.

Over the next couple of months, her feelings blossomed. She helped him with his English, and he helped her with her Spanish. She learned he had moved to the United States from Mexico City the year before after his grandfather, who had raised him, had passed away.

Initially, their relationship remained a secret from her family. Rebekah's father was the pastor of a mega church in Atlanta, and he had certain expectations where his children were concerned. They did not include sneaking around with a young man who didn't have a college education, had hardly any money, and didn't attend church on a regular basis.

During the week, they talked on the phone late into the night. On the weekends, their clandestine meetings were orchestrated with the help of her friends. She would say she was going to the movies or over to a friend's house, when in fact, she met secretly with Rafael.

When her father found out, he grounded her and insisted on meeting Rafael. She thought the meeting had gone well until her father informed her she was not to see him ever again.

Unfortunately for him, his refusal to approve of Rafael only made Rebekah want to see him more. Their times apart were torture, their moments together precious. She distinctly remembered when everything changed…

* * *

REBEKAH AND RAFAEL were in the back seat of her car, parked up at Stone Mountain Park. The windows were fogged from the heat of their heavy petting clashing with the low temperature of the cool fall night.

She sat astride him, topless, as he kissed and touched her.

With reluctance, Rafael tore his mouth away from hers. "It's time to go," he said, his voice thick and rough. "If we keep this up, I won't be able to stop."

"No." She clung to him, burying her face in his neck, wrapping her arms tight around him.

"Rebekah, we already talked about this. If you do not get home at a reasonable hour, your father will be suspicious and we will never get to see each other because he will never let you out of his sight."

"I don't want to go," she said, her voice muffled against his neck. It got harder and harder to leave him after each stolen moment together.

"*Ángel*," he said, tilting her head up with gentle fingers, "we leave now, okay? And I will see you next week."

Reluctantly, she sat up. "I hate this," Rebekah said tremulously after she had slipped her shirt over her head.

"Rebekah, please, do not do this. You know this is hard for me too, but it is not forever. It is only for a short time."

"I don't want to keep hiding."

"I know, *mi amor*. Me, either. But you must obey your father."

"I just want to be with you." On the verge of tears, her lower lip quivered. "I love you." She blurted the words without thinking.

"Rebekah—"

"I do!"

"You do not know what you are saying. You are still very young. How could you love a man like me? I have nothing—I cannot give you the life your father has."

"In January I'll be eighteen—I'll be a woman, and I know about love. I love you, Rafe. I don't care about money and all that stuff." Sitting back on his thighs, she lifted her tear-filled eyes toward his, her heart thudding heavily in her chest. "Do you love me?" She hated the neediness of the question, but she had to know.

He cupped her face in his big hands. "*Si, mi amor. Te amo demasiado. Estoy loco por ti.*" He had told her he loved her too much, and that he was crazy about her.

"Promise?" Tears spilled from her eyes. He brushed them away with the pads of his thumbs.

"*Para siempre.*" Forever.

RAFAEL SETTLED onto the stool at the hotel bar in Manhattan. He'd been fortunate to get a last minute flight from Atlanta. Flying out tonight had been preferable to his original plan to fly out in the morning. It would save him some time, which meant he would be able to get back sooner to spend time with his son.

The corners of his mouth lifted into a bittersweet smile. He already loved him fiercely, as if he had known him all his life.

Both his parents had died an untimely death while in their twenties. They'd been teenagers when Rafael was born, and they'd lived a life of crime that eventually caught up with them when they crossed the drug dealer for whom they had worked. He didn't want Ricardo to know anything about that kind of life. He would give him everything he never had growing up and teach him to be a man in the same way he had been taught by his grandfather.

If everything went well tomorrow, he would be back in Atlanta by tomorrow night.

"What'll you have?" the bartender asked, a young man with skin the color of rich mahogany.

"Bourbon. Straight. And a menu." He could tell by the light of recognition in his eyes, the younger man knew who he was, but he said nothing as he handed him a menu.

"Excuse me," a sultry voice said. A buxom brunette stood nearby. "Aren't you a wrestler? Umm…what was it…*La Sombra*, right?"

He didn't doubt she knew exactly who he was. Some women had a way of pretending they didn't know who he was so they wouldn't seem too zealous in their approach.

"That's right." He took in the plunging neckline, which showed off her humungous breasts. She had a narrow waist and wide hips. She wasn't bad-looking, either, but she smelled like she'd soaked in a barrel of perfume.

"Can I have your autograph?" she practically purred, pouting her ruby-red lips and sticking her chest out even more—as if he couldn't already see her enormous breasts. Her well-manicured fingers retrieved a little notebook from her tiny beaded purse and placed it in front of him with a pen.

"Who am I writing it to?"

"Connie," she whispered, pressing her chest against his bicep. He didn't even have to work for it. It was almost too easy.

Rafael pretended not to notice the pressure on his arm and scribbled the note as quickly as possible. "Here you go."

Connie took the notebook and pen and slipped both into her purse without taking her eyes from his face. "Are you staying here?" she asked, giving him a come-hither look, which, instead of enticing him, made his flesh crawl.

"No," he lied.

Connie pouted again and stepped back. "I am," she said coyly. "Room twelve-eleven, in case you're interested." Rafael watched as she sashayed out the door of the bar.

"Must be nice," the bartender murmured.

"It can be a nuisance sometimes," Rafael said, flipping open the menu. It was late, and he was starving.

"I'd love to have that kind of problem."

No, you would not, Rafael thought grimly.

* * *

AT TWENTY-TWO, Rafael was big, strong, and a good fighter. When Marty took him under his wing, he went from no-holds-barred underground fighting to the wrestling amateur league. By this time, he and Rebekah had been married a year. The money he made barely supported them. Rebekah hadn't liked the violence of underground wrestling, having to deal with all his cuts, bruises, and black eyes after each bout. She liked amateur wrestling even less, because Rafael had to travel often, leaving her behind in the motel room they rented weekly.

She offered to get a job so he wouldn't have to be gone as much, but Rafael wouldn't hear about it. No wife of his would work. He would take care of her.

While on one of his trips, he was taken by surprise when she called to tell him she was going to Atlanta. She explained that since he was gone for weeks at a time, she would stay with her parents for awhile.

For Rafael, it indicated her unhappiness, which, in turn, was an embarrassing blow to his ego. Their relationship became more strained. They barely talked, and when they did, it was only to argue. He accused her of leaving him, which she vehemently denied.

He flew back to Atlanta, hoping to convince her to return with him, but he could see she was becoming more entrenched in her life there. He had no doubt her mind was being poisoned against him, and she seemed to enjoy the comfort afforded by her father's money. They were living separate lives.

When he hit the road again for his bouts in California, he missed her, but their conversations became fewer and far between. The biggest mistake he had ever made happened just a few weeks after he left. He had won his matches, and he called Rebekah to tell her the news, but she wasn't at home. Hours later, she still hadn't returned his call, and he had felt dejected.

Marty would sometimes rent a hotel suite so the six wrestlers he managed could celebrate after their matches. Tonight, they'd won a lot of money, so there was more food, more alcohol, and more women. Normally, Rafael would go back to his own room, but tonight, he didn't want to be alone, and he needed a distraction from his thoughts.

There were at least two groupies—or ring rats, as they were called—for each wrestler. While most of the women were wrestling groupies, a few had a professional air about them.

"Hey, youngblood." That was The Smasher, an older black wrestler with a gravelly voice who grew up in the seventies and spoke as if he were still living in that decade. He clapped Rafael on the shoulder. "There's a whole lot of fine tail here tonight. You're the star of this show. Take your pick." He waved his hand in a kingly gesture, offering permission for Rafael to choose a woman.

"No, thanks." Rafael started to walk away, but The Smasher slipped his arm around his neck and held him in place.

"You need to stop all this sulking now. Time to get with the program." The putrid odor of bad breath mixed with heavy doses of beer and hard liquor drifted under Rafael's nose. "That girl ain't thinking about you."

Rafael stiffened. He didn't bother to point out Rebekah wasn't just any "girl." She was his wife. It made no difference to the other men. They still teased him. Half of them were married with a wife and kids at home, but they didn't let it stop their fun.

"She all the way in Atlanta," The Smasher continued. "She probably got her one of them college men by now. Or you best believe Daddy's done set her up with one of them fine Christian men in his congregation."

The same thoughts had crossed his mind. Her father had never thought he was good enough and had said no when Rafael asked for Rebekah's hand in marriage. So what would keep him from pointing out all the eligible young men available and capable of providing for his daughter in a traditional way?

Angry, Rafael shoved the other man's arm off his shoulder. The Smasher backed up, laughing as he did so. "Whoa, now," he said. "Don't get mad at me for speaking the truth."

"That's my wife you're talking about," Rafael snarled.

The Smasher looped his arms around the necks of two women standing nearby. "Listen here, this is America. You ain't in Mexico no more, *hombre*. In America, you can have anything you want. *Anything*." He pulled the two women closer to emphasize his point. They giggled. "If a tree falls on a bear in the forest…no, wait a minute…if a bear pisses in the woods and no one is around…no…ah, what the hell! You know what I'm trying to say. She ain't here, so what she don't know can't hurt you." With an exaggerated, drunken wink, The Smasher lumbered off toward one of the bedrooms with both women.

Sick of what he saw and trying to escape his gloominess, Rafael headed out onto the patio for some fresh air. He was out there for a few minutes when he heard movement behind him. A bottle of beer appeared, connected to a female hand. He took the beer and turned to face the woman attached to the arm.

She had a round face, large brown eyes, and short, dark hair. "Hi," she said. "I'm Marisol."

She didn't look like the typical groupie. Her hair wasn't teased to the heights of small buildings, her face wasn't padded with too much makeup, and her body was twice as covered as the other women inside.

"Thank you."

"You're from Mexico City, right?" she asked.

He nodded.

"That's where my parents are from. I was born here in the States, but I visit every chance I get."

"What are you doing here, Marisol?"

"I'm here with a friend." She rolled her eyes. "She's a fan of one of the other wrestlers. I can't remember his name. Mind if I stay out here with you?"

"No."

He brought out two of the dining room table chairs, and they sat outside and talked for some time. Later, when all hell broke loose, all he could think was that he should have never gone to the suite in the first place. He never even touched Marisol, or any other woman there, but the fallout was as devastating as if he had slept with them.

Two reporters for a national tabloid had been at the party that night with hidden cameras. Their assignment was to shed light on the wrestling industry and the athletes who traveled around, leaving wives and children at home. The exposé uncovered the drug use, drinking, and sex rampant in the industry.

When the story broke, it was all over the news. He was still traveling at the time and called Rebekah immediately. As one of the more popular wrestlers, his name and image featured prominently in the piece, and there was no mistaking the distinctive Aztec tattoo on his left bicep. The colorful illustration depicted Mixcoatl, the Aztec god of war and the hunt.

He had explained to Rebekah that he hadn't done anything wrong, but she hadn't believed him. Eventually, she refused to take any more of his calls. He continued to call until one night her father answered and told him to leave his daughter alone. She could do better than a liar and an adulterer. Rebekah sent a message to him through her father: *She wanted a divorce.*

After he hung up, he was in a daze. Then, the consequences of his actions buried him under a weight of anger. With a roar, he attacked the hotel room. He broke apart the dresser and smashed the mirror above it with his fist. He never saw the blood or felt the pain of the shards imbedded in his hand.

The noise finally penetrated the revelry of music and laughter in the other room of the suite. Wrestlers poured into the room, and he tried to smash them too.

"Hold on, youngblood. Save it for the ring, son."

He was young, he was strong, and he had the adrenaline of anger and pain pumping through his veins. It took all five of them to restrain him. The room was in a shambles. Someone called Marty, and he rushed over to the hotel right away.

Marty lectured him for a long time. "Use your anger in the ring," he said.

That's exactly what Rafael did.

He was unmatched in the arena of amateur fighting, and the bad publicity only helped his bad boy image. Within months, his persona skyrocketed, and Marty was able to ink a lucrative deal with World Wrestling Entertainment.

He had found success, but he wasn't happy. He threw himself into the lifestyle, taking his pleasure from different women and drinking to drown his sorrows. The only bright spot in his life was when he was in the ring. His fans helped him through those dark days. Before each entrance, the audience chanted his name in excited frenzy.

"*La Sombra! La Sombra!*"

His marriage may have died, but his wrestling career had just been born.

CHAPTER 5

"*R*icky, come on, let's go!"

"Coming, Mom!" Ricardo bounded down the stairs.

They were both freshly showered and changed into clean clothes after spending the day at Zoo Atlanta. Rebekah watched as he lifted the paper sack of vegetables she'd picked from the garden to take to her parents' house.

She wore a maxi dress, the lovely print flattering against her dark skin. Her long, thick hair hung in loose waves past her shoulders.

"You look pretty, Mom," Ricardo volunteered.

"Thank you, sweetie." Rebekah leaned down to kiss his cheek. "Ready?"

"Yep!"

She pulled open the door. Rafael was on the other side, standing with his hand poised to ring the doorbell.

"Dad!" Ricardo squealed.

"What are you doing here?"

He quirked a brow, his warm gaze sliding over her sun-kissed bare arms and shoulders, exposed by the spaghetti straps of the dress. His appreciative gaze lingered a fraction too long at the spot where the dress dipped over her ample breasts before falling in loose folds to swirl around her calves. A tingling sensation surfaced in the pit of her stomach and her breasts tightened under the weight of his blatant male perusal.

"I came to see if I could take the two of you to dinner."

Rebekah couldn't help staring at him. He looked good enough to eat in a pair of snug-fitting jeans and a white polo shirt that contrasted nicely against his swarthy skin.

"We already have plans," Ricardo said. "We're going to Grandma and Grandpa's house. Wanna come?"

"Ricky, I don't think—"

"I would love to." Rafael's words sliced across her protesting. "I'm so hungry I could eat a horse."

"Grandpa says Grandma cooks enough food to feed the entire state of Georgia."

Rafael flashed a heart-stopping smile. "There shouldn't be any problem with me joining you for dinner, then, should there?"

"Nope."

"Rafe, I don't think this is a good idea," Rebekah said, finally able to squeeze in a word. She was almost certain the two of them were conspiring against her.

"And why's that?" Rafael asked.

"You know why," Rebekah said through gritted teeth, conscious of Ricardo's curious gaze during their conversation. "I wouldn't want to surprise my parents with unexpected company. You were supposed to be gone a couple of days."

"My plans changed. I came back early because I wanted to spend time with my son."

"You can't expect me to just spring this on my parents at the last minute."

"No, I don't. You can give them a call first and warn them I'm coming. How's that?"

Rebekah sighed heavily. "Let's just go, okay?"

There was no point in arguing. Although his face appeared friendly, he wouldn't budge, and it seemed almost petty to deprive him of time with Ricardo when he stood right in front of them.

The three climbed into Rafael's rented Lexus SUV. Once she was comfortably buckled into the tan leather seats, Rebekah called her parents. The phone rang four times and went to voicemail. She left a quick message.

"This is a really bad idea," Rebekah murmured. She kept her voice low so Ricardo couldn't hear her in the back seat.

"I disagree." Rafael glanced at her before returning his eyes to the road. "They might as well get used to having me back in their lives."

"You could have waited."

"Never put off until tomorrow what you can do today."

"You're getting a kick out of this, aren't you?" Rebekah fumed, folding her arms across her chest.

"I have to admit, I can't wait to see the look on your father's face when he finds out I'm back in your life." His cool gray eyes locked with hers, and Rebekah felt a shiver run down her spine. Her eyes skittered away from his to look out the passenger window. How could she still be so attracted to him?

Years ago, he had caused her to behave in a manner completely outside the scope of her character. She had disobeyed her parents by sneaking around behind their backs. She had run off and gotten married to a man they vehemently disapproved of. Deep down, she was terrified her lapse in judgment was not limited to the idiocy of youth.

"I was going to tell them tonight."

"You still can. I'll be right there to help you with the explanation."

That was the problem, and he very well knew it. Rebekah

closed her eyes against the passing scenery. It was going to be a long night.

* * *

TWENTY-FIVE MINUTES LATER, the SUV pulled into the driveway of the Jamison house. It was a large, traditional two-story home in the Eagle's Landing country club community located twenty-four miles south of Atlanta. The seven bedroom house sat on a premium lot with a professionally landscaped yard overlooking the golf course.

Dr. Adam Jamison, Sr. was the pastor of the largest Baptist congregation in the Southeast. The community where he and his wife lived was 3,000 acres of luxury living, which included a 27-hole golf course, eight lighted tennis courts, three swimming pools, and fitness facilities.

Ricardo ran ahead of them with his package of vegetables to the front door and let himself in. Rebekah followed more slowly, dreading the pending conversation with her parents. For his part, Rafael appeared completely unconcerned, which grated on her nerves. It wasn't fair he should be so calm and cool when she was coming undone like a loosened spool of string.

"Grandma! Grandpa!" she heard her son bellow on his way to the kitchen. His sneakered feet slapped loudly against the marble tile as he bolted through the two-story foyer.

This house had once been his home. They had lived in the two bedrooms and bath in the basement after she and Rafael split, but they'd had unlimited access to the top floors. After working part-time and earning her degree in education, it was another year before Rebekah had saved enough to put a down payment on the three-bedroom fixer-upper she now owned in the city of Stone Mountain.

Nowadays, the apartment downstairs was used as temporary housing for anyone who was experiencing financial difficulties.

When it was empty, out-of-town visitors to the church had the option to stay there instead of a hotel.

As Rafael closed the door behind them, Rebekah could hear her mother laughing. "I can't wait to see your surprise," she said with her singsong Caribbean accent.

"Please, let me do the talking," Rebekah said softly to Rafael.

"As you wish."

Shortly thereafter, her mother appeared wearing an apron over her slacks, being led by Ricardo, whose little hand pulled her forward. She had her eyes closed but was smiling, taking obvious delight in his excitement. Her waist-length hair was pulled back from her face in a thick braid. Her light-colored skin indicated her biracial heritage.

"Okay, Grandma, open your eyes."

Rebekah pasted a smile on her face, determined not to let her mother know how deeply the events of the past day had affected her. Both of her parents had seen her at her worst after the breakup of her marriage, and she knew how much they had hurt for her during that ordeal. She didn't want them to be concerned about her. She was older and wiser and could handle the situation with Rafael on her own without assistance.

"Ta-da! This is my dad!" Ricardo's boisterous behavior continued unrestrained. It was almost funny. He had no idea the enormity of the unfolding events. For him, it was simply exciting, and he wanted his father and grandmother to meet.

Mrs. Jamison's eyes flicked from Rebekah to Rafael in a face drained of color.

"Mom, your mouth is open," Rebekah said.

Stirred from her daze, her mother quickly shut her mouth. She cleared her throat. "Well, I...this really is a surprise." She smiled weakly.

"He's a wrestler," Ricardo added proudly.

"I'm sorry this had to happen like this." Rebekah walked over to her mother and gave her a hug. "It was a surprise for me, too.

I didn't want to spring it on you, but no one answered the phone when I called earlier to let you know I was bringing company."

"Yes, well, I was in the kitchen finishing up dinner, and your father was taking a nap. I heard the phone ring, but...I will certainly be more vigilant about answering it in the future." Mrs. Jamison's brown eyes roved over her daughter's face with concern. "Are you all right?" She brought her thin fingers up to Rebekah's shoulder.

"Of course. Why wouldn't I be?" She could pull it off. She could convince them everything was fine.

Mrs. Jamison seemed to want to say more, but she stopped herself. She looked past her daughter to Rafael. "Welcome, Rafael. It's been a long time."

"Yes, it has." Rafael came forward and clasped his mother-in-law's hand in both of his. "How is it possible that you've become even more beautiful?"

"Well," she said, her cheeks blooming with color, "that's very kind of you."

"I only speak the truth."

Rebekah thought it would be better for Rafael to save his charm for her father. While her mother had not been happy about their elopement and had agreed with her father regarding the suitability of Rafael for their daughter, she had not approved of keeping Ricardo a secret. Nonetheless, she understood what Rebekah had gone through and had supported her all these years.

When she and Rafael got married after her father had denied permission to Rafael, he declared Rafael had stolen his daughter from him. In the years since then, his dislike of Rafael had never wavered.

"Is that my grandson I hear?" Her father's booming voice, which had the same pitch of a blues singer and was the perfect timbre for a pastor of a mega church, could be heard from upstairs. Dr. Jamison came into view on the landing above. "Is that my grand—" The words died in his throat, his right foot hovering above the top stair.

"Hi, Dad." It was all she could think of to say at the moment.

"Grandpa, this is *my* dad. He's a wrestler. His name is *La Sombra*."

Her father looked like he'd just seen a ghost. "I know who your father is."

"Rebekah tried to call us, dear, but we didn't answer the phone." She could hear the nervous strain in her mother's voice.

Dr. Jamison descended the curved staircase very slowly.

"I'm sorry I couldn't give you more notice, but Ricky asked Rafe to join us for dinner."

"Is everything okay?" her father asked when he arrived at the bottom.

"Everything is fine, Dad."

"Dr. Jamison."

"Rafael."

The stilted greeting between the two of them increased the tension already heavy in the air.

Mrs. Jamison took Ricardo's hand. "Let's finish getting dinner ready. You have your job to do."

"I have to set the table," Ricardo said, looking up at his father.

"That's a very important job," Rafael told him.

Ricardo nodded and then disappeared with his grandmother.

The moment they were out of earshot, Rebekah's father turned on Rafael. His dark face was filled with anger. "What do you think you're doing here in my house? I told you a long time ago you're not welcome here."

"Dad, please."

"I would have thought that would have changed by now." Rafael's voice was quiet, but she knew he was nowhere near

41

intimidated by her father. Although her father wasn't a small man, Rafael was wider and taller than him by several inches.

"Nothing has changed," Dr. Jamison said. "You stole my daughter away, and then when you were done having your fun, you broke her heart, and I had to be there to pick up the pieces."

"Dad, stop it."

"Dr. Jamison, I came here to spend time with the son I never knew I had."

"Leave Ricardo out of it. My daughter's done a good job with him."

"Yes, she has. But now I'm here, despite the fact that all of you conspired to—"

"Stop it!" Rebekah's voice came out louder than intended. They may have heard her in the dining room. She drew in a shaky breath. "Dad, he's Ricky's father, and Ricky invited him. He wants to have Rafe here. For Ricky's sake, would the two of you just try to be civil for the next couple of hours so we can get through this meal? I don't care how you do it, but pretend you like each other. I don't want him upset."

The scowls on their faces didn't diminish, but at least they were no longer picking at one another.

"By the way, Dad. I have something else to tell you." She decided there was no better time than the present to tell her father the rest of the news. "Rafe and I are still married."

His head whipped in her direction. "What are you talking about?" She explained everything to him and watched as he ran his hand down his face. "This is terrible," he said.

"Dad, the divorce is just a formality."

"I'm not just talking about the divorce," her father said. "I wish...I wish we'd answered the phone earlier."

His voice was filled with such gloom she couldn't help but think he was overreacting. "Dad, it's really not that big of a deal. It's one dinner."

"That's not what I'm talking about, Rebekah. I invited

someone else to dinner earlier today. In light of what you just said, this is going to be very, very awkward."

As if on cue, the doorbell rang, and they all turned toward the door. Without explaining his last words, Dr. Jamison crossed the foyer and opened it. In walked Carlton Smith, one of the deacons of the church.

"Good evening," Carlton said, smiling.

Oh no.

Could the evening get any worse? Now she had the unsavory task of introducing the man she was dating to the man she was married to.

CHAPTER 6

"*R*icky's father?"

Carlton Smith's affable smile wavered and his face reddened when the introductions were made. Nonetheless, he stuck out his hand in greeting.

With immense effort, Rafael shook Carlton's hand, but he couldn't resist squeezing it a little more than necessary. He had no intention of becoming friends with the man who was sleeping with his wife and who might very well be a surrogate father to his son.

Rebekah's gaze narrowed when Carlton flinched, but Rafael gave nothing away, looking coolly down at her as if he couldn't understand Carlton's reaction.

* * *

WHEN THE FOUR were on their way to the dining room, Carlton held Rebekah back with a hand on her arm.

"What's going on here, Rebekah?" He had a frown on his pale face.

"I'm sorry. I didn't know he was coming tonight. I didn't want you to find out like this. He arrived in town yesterday."

"Yesterday! Why didn't you call me?"

The steady pulse of a headache pounded through her skull. She was not in the mood to explain her actions to Carlton or anyone else. If it weren't for Rafael, there would be no need for explanations. It was his fault for bulldozing his way back into her life without a word of warning. She'd barely had twenty-four hours to get used to the idea before he returned to dominate the weekly dinners she enjoyed with her parents.

"Because I thought I had time to let you know what was going on. My father failed to mention he'd invited you to dinner tonight. Up until you came through the door, I had no idea you were joining us."

"It was sort of last minute." He took her hand, but she slipped hers out of his grasp. "I can't touch you now?"

"It's not that." Rebekah bit her lip. "Things are a little complicated."

"Complicated how?" Looking uneasy, Carlton buried his hands in his pockets. He probably thought she and Rafael planned to rekindle their relationship. He didn't know the half of it.

"Complicated in that—well, I might as well go on and tell you. Rafe told me he and I are still married."

There was stunned silence. "Is this a joke?"

Funny he should have the same reaction she had. "Look at my face. Do you see me laughing?"

"Are you certain? Does he have proof?"

"I haven't seen any proof yet, but he has no reason to lie. Of course our marriage will be verified, but for now, all I have is his word."

"This isn't happening," Carlton said with a disbelieving shake of his head. "You can't still be married to this guy."

"Unfortunately, I am."

"How?"

Rebekah explained the courthouse mishap that managed to keep her married to Rafael.

Carlton ran his fingers through his sandy-blond hair. "What now?"

"We're getting a divorce just as soon as we can get the papers drawn up."

"And Ricardo?"

"Well, that's another complication. We have to work out custody, but I assured Rafe he would have full access to his son. I don't have any intention of keeping them apart anymore. Ricky already practically worships the ground he walks on."

"Is he going to pay child support? Alimony? He's well off, so he can afford it."

"My only concern is Ricardo. I don't want anything from Rafe." Rebekah took a deep breath. "We haven't talked much about any of that. There hasn't been time. Right now, the plan is for him and Ricky to get to know each other better, and we'll figure the rest out later."

"He has a lot of money, Rebekah. You could be a very wealthy woman in this divorce."

Rebekah bristled. "I don't want his money, Carlton. I don't want anything from him. And that would be very hypocritical of me, considering I hate everything about the lifestyle that helped him get that money."

Carlton shrugged. "I wouldn't be so quick to walk away from it if I were you. California is a community property state, and he probably expects to have to pay in this divorce."

His mercenary pronouncements made Rebekah uncomfortable. "Thank you for that information," she said in a stiff voice. "I have an appointment with an attorney tomorrow, and I'm sure he'll give me good advice about what I should do."

"How do you feel about him?"

The forthright question threw her off balance, but she

couldn't fault Carlton for asking it. In truth, she had to acknowledge she was still attracted to Rafael. He was probably wondering where they stood now that her husband had resurfaced in her life.

"I want him to have a good relationship with Ricky." Like a politician, she deftly avoided answering the question. Her next words were more difficult. "I...think you and I should put the brakes on dating for awhile. I'd feel better once I'm officially divorced."

She and Carlton had been dating for a few months, and while she thought he could be husband material, she was hesitant to make their relationship an exclusive one. Carlton had assured her he was not interested in anyone else and wanted a commitment, but he'd eventually stopped pushing.

He threw a look of displeasure in her direction. "This is a crazy situation, but you're right. It would be best if we halted our relationship for awhile. I wouldn't want anyone at church to know I would knowingly date a married woman. How long will this be necessary?"

"It shouldn't take long. A couple of months or so should do it."

Carlton muttered something about Jesus and then his face broke into a tight smile. "I'll pray the attorneys move quickly."

"Dinner is ready."

They both swung their heads toward Rafael. He stood there, big and brawny, his glacial stare trained on Carlton. He'd obviously heard Carlton's comment. Without another word, the three made their way down the hallway into the dining room.

An oval table that seated six sat in the middle of the room. Rebekah's mother had outdone herself again. Serving dishes were filled with braised oxtails, spicy curry chicken, peas and rice, rice cooked in coconut milk, fried plantains, and coleslaw. The pleasing aromas stimulated Rebekah's appetite and temporarily distracted her from the undercurrent of tension in the room. She hadn't eaten since she and Ricardo had lunch during their trip to the zoo.

Rebekah watched as Ricardo stood idly until he saw where his father would sit and plunked down in the chair next to him. If she wanted indisputable proof that she shouldn't have kept them apart, tonight she received it. Her heart constricted as she watched her son even mimic his father's movements.

Both of Rebekah's parents sat at each end of the table. Carlton sat to her right, and across from him sat Rafael with Ricardo next to him.

The meal progressed with a fair amount of conversation, mostly dominated by Carlton and her father as they discussed activities at church. Ricardo shared what he had seen at the zoo earlier. Every now and again, Rebekah would look up to find Rafael watching her. Other times, he would have his eyes on Carlton. He stared at the other man with such undisguised hostility, she half-expected him to start a brawl in the middle of dinner.

She was relieved when each person at the table had a slice of her mother's mango cake with buttercream icing in front of them, indicating the evening would soon come to a close.

"When are you leaving to go back to California?" Carlton asked.

Rafael pushed his empty dessert plate aside and leaned forward on crossed forearms. "Just as soon as Ricardo and Rebekah can get packed up and ready to go."

A morsel of cake lodged in Rebekah's throat as Carlton slid his questioning gaze toward her. After a little cough, she picked up her glass and swallowed some punch.

"What does he mean by that?" Carlton asked.

"You're going to California?" Her mother's voice sounded almost panicked.

Rebekah cleared her throat and proceeded to answer the

questions right after she shot a dirty look diagonally across the table at Rafael. His stone-faced visage gave nothing away.

"I planned to tell you," she said, glancing around the table. "Ricky and I are going to California for the rest of the summer so he and Rafe can spend time together."

"We're going to build sand castles at the beach!" her son interjected with a grin. He pushed aside his dessert plate and then leaned his forearms on the table like his father.

"Is that really wise?" Dr. Jamison asked.

"Why wouldn't it be?" With a dart of her eyes, Rebekah indicated Ricardo seated across the table from her.

"I hope you know what you're doing," Carlton said tightly. He slammed his napkin onto the table. "I don't understand why you have to spend the next couple of months over there."

A knot of unease manifested itself in Rebekah's midsection. She watched as Rafael narrowed his gaze on Carlton.

"You have a problem with my wife and my son joining me in California?"

Carlton swallowed, realizing too late he'd made a mistake. The dangerous glint in Rafael's eyes signaled his displeasure. "Obviously, it's none of my business—"

"Obviously."

Carlton's back straightened, and Rebekah speculated he was about to say something that would so infuriate Rafael he just might reach across the table and tear him limb from limb. Carlton had no idea what he was doing if he thought challenging Rafael was a good idea.

She didn't think Rafael would initiate a fight in the middle of her parents' dining room in front of their son, but she couldn't be certain. He had a temper, and he outweighed Carlton by at least seventy-five pounds, most of which were muscle. On other turf, he may very well have backed Carlton against a wall to make sure he understood in no uncertain terms that he'd overstepped his bounds.

"This isn't the time or place for this conversation," she said. She pushed her chair back without rising. "It's getting late. We should leave."

After her pronouncement, a chorus of voices erupted across the table. Carlton muttered his agreement, looking away from Rafael as if he finally realized he ran the risk of getting squashed underfoot like an ant as soon as Rafael had the opportunity. Her mother mumbled something about packing up leftovers to take home. Her father mentioned he was looking forward to next week's dinner.

All the while, Rebekah kept her eyes on Rafael, and his remained on her. A tremor of awareness shimmied down her spine. She knew what she saw in those cool gray depths. Through the use of the word "my," he had staked his claim. He hadn't just claimed Ricky. He had claimed her too.

For some peculiar reason, a small part of her liked it.

CHAPTER 7

$\mathcal{T}$he drive back to Stone Mountain was a quiet one. Ricardo fell asleep, so when they pulled up in the driveway of the house, Rafael went around to the back to lift him into his arms.

From the back seat, Rebekah grabbed the canvas tote with leftovers her mother had packed.

"I'll take him upstairs," Rafael said once they'd entered the house.

In his son's bedroom, he removed Ricardo's shoes and socks before placing him under the covers. He stared down at him for a moment, his heart filled with heaviness at the thought of what he'd missed over the years.

Driving home with his wife and son in the car and bringing Ricardo up to bed had seemed like the most natural thing in the world. The magnitude of what he'd lost because of his lapse in judgment came crashing down on him with acute force. He ran his fingers over his son's thick curls, then bent down to brush a kiss against his forehead.

He had indicated his willingness to share custody, but

summers and alternating holidays were no longer a palatable schedule.

Rafael entered the kitchen just as Rebekah straightened from tucking the last of the containers into the refrigerator.

"Is he still asleep?" she asked.

"Yes. He hardly moved when I put him in bed."

"He's probably out for the rest of the night. It's been a long day, and he sleeps soundly."

"Takes after his father," Rafael said with a smile. Rebekah used to tease him that if someone broke into their motel room, they would both be killed because he wouldn't hear her screams for help.

She didn't return his smile. She licked her lips nervously, and his eyes followed the movement with interest.

"Rafe," she began, "we need to set some ground rules if this is going to work. We've both been living separate lives, and we have to respect each other's space and make sure there are boundaries."

"What kind of boundaries?" he asked in a suspicious voice.

"Relationship boundaries, for one. Your behavior with Carlton tonight was…a bit much."

"*He* was a bit much."

"You have to understand, it was a shock for him to find out what he did. And it's not as if you and I are really married."

"The law says we are."

"You know what I mean. We're not married in the sense that we've been living together as husband and wife. Would you consider treating Carlton with a little more respect and stop directing so much animosity toward him? He's a really nice person."

"What are you suggesting? That he and I become friends?" Rafael asked cynically.

"I know it's not going to happen right now, but I think you should at least be open to the idea."

He didn't like that she was looking at him as if he was the bad guy. Granted, years had passed, but seeing Carlton had awakened something primitive inside him. He didn't like the thought of another man in the life of his wife and son.

"Are you going to have this same conversation with the good deacon? That hug he gave you before we left your parents' house was meant to provoke me."

He'd watched in simmering rage as Carlton held her in an embrace, his arms around her waist, pulling her close when he, Rafael, couldn't even touch her.

"It was an innocent hug. It's not as if he kissed me in front of you."

"Lucky for him, or he'd be in the hospital right now. He was trying to push my buttons because of what I said at the dinner table."

"He doesn't think like that."

"He's a man. Trust me, he thinks like that." Her defense of Carlton had him on edge and made him want to pummel him even more. A trace of anger slipped into his voice when he said, "You're as much my wife today as you were the day I married you. Until that changes, the good deacon needs to keep his distance."

Carlton would be wise to stay the hell away from his wife— and his son, for that matter. Those were *his* rules.

His jealousy was irrational, but that didn't lessen the strength of it. He certainly hadn't lived the life of a monk, yet he couldn't cast off the thoughts that overtook him. She was still his wife. *His.* He hated the thought of another man touching her, getting close to her, having her.

"I see you haven't lost your possessive streak."

"I'm only possessive about what's mine."

"So am I. Lot of good it did me."

"That's it," Rafael ground out. He invaded her personal space by placing one hand on the counter behind her. She stared up at him, wide-eyed. "While we're talking about boundaries, let's start with no more bringing up the past. I told you I never slept with those women."

"There were pictures."

He cursed in Spanish, and then he took a deep breath to calm his temper and think coherently enough to continue the conversation in English. "Yes, there were pictures, and I'm not saying it wasn't me. I made a mistake, but I swear to you, nothing happened."

"Oh, right, you were out on the patio *talking* while everyone else was drinking, doing drugs, and having sex."

"Is it really that hard for you to believe I could be there and not participate? I guess since I'm not one of the Saint Jamisons, who, by the way, thought it fit to keep my son from me—"

"Don't talk about my family!"

"Why not?" he said tersely. "We both know I've never met the criteria to be welcomed into your family."

"Even if I believe you—which I don't—don't try to pretend you didn't want to have your fun like the rest of your buddies. If not, then why were you there in the first place? You expect me to believe you were just standing around, all innocent, just *looking*? They had to block out parts of the photos because some of those women didn't have any clothes on!"

"Rebekah—"

"Those pictures were horrible. Everyone knew. It was humiliating."

He heard the tremor in her voice, could see the pain in her dark brown eyes. "If I could change what happened, I would," he said, the muscles in his throat clenched tight with regret. "I've never forgiven myself for hurting you."

* * *

SHE COULD SEE the regret in his face at what they had lost. She felt it, too, and her heart broke all over again. Perhaps his actions years ago weren't as callous and uncaring as she'd originally thought. She had been so hurt when the tabloid story came out, knowing *her* husband was in those photos. She had worried about him and the fighting, missed him so much when he traveled, yet it seemed he hadn't missed her at all. He had been too busy partying with the other wrestlers and the slew of women who followed them around.

"We have to figure out a way to get along," he said. "At least for Ricardo's sake."

"I know." Talking about the pain of the past had drained her.

He reached out and touched her hair.

"What are you doing?" she asked in a panic-stricken voice. She couldn't get away from him. She was more or less blocked in by the refrigerator to her right and his muscular arm to the left.

"Piece of lint," he responded, showing her. "You seem…what is the word…skittish?"

Her heart rate started a steady acceleration. "You're too close, and it's making me uncomfortable. Would you step back?"

Rapid fluttering like that of tiny butterflies settled in the pit of her stomach. How could she want him when she still bore the wounds of their ruined marriage?

"Why would you be uncomfortable? I'm not uncomfortable around you."

"You're not the one crowded against the kitchen counter by a giant wrestler."

The corners of his mouth lifted slightly in an amused smile before he stepped back. In an ironic reversal, she missed his closeness. A knowing smile stretched fully across his face. He considered her with a long, appraising look.

"What?"

"Do you really like him?"

"I think we need to continue our conversation about boundaries, and we should include respecting each other's privacy."

"I have nothing to hide."

"Neither do I."

"Then tell me about Deacon Carlton."

"No." She and Carlton had never been intimate. Because of his position in the church, he remained celibate.

"I just want to know about my competition."

Rebekah swallowed, apprehension settling in her gut. "There is no competition. Our marriage is over."

"It's not over until the papers are signed. Until then, you're still my wife."

"Don't remind me. The sooner we get this over with, the better."

"So you can rush off to the good deacon?"

"I won't ask you about your affairs, so don't ask me about mine!" She only took one step before he grabbed her arm and hauled her back around to face him.

The hard collision with the wall of his chest knocked the air from her lungs. She put up a hand to push away from him, but his arm entwined around her waist like a steel brace and trapped her against him. Everywhere they touched, warmth seeped from his body into hers.

Her gaze shifted to his sensuous mouth when he lowered his face toward her. Her nose recognized and welcomed his masculine smell.

"Let's get one thing straight," he said. His calm voice held a threatening undertone. "There will be no 'affairs.' While you're my wife, no one comes near you."

"I think—"

"Do *not* try me, Rebekah." His face became a hardened mask of anger. "Unless you have a pressing desire to see every bone in the good deacon's body broken—or any other man, for that matter—I suggest you give him a call and make sure he understands your relationship is over until further notice. If you don't call him, I will, and he won't like my conversation."

A frisson of apprehension snaked down her spine at the threat, but she couldn't deny also feeling a trickle of excitement at his possessiveness. He was as big and strong as an ox and capable of successful follow-through on his words.

"I've already talked to Carlton about it and he understands." She surprised herself with her next words. "That goes for you, too, by the way. You're still my husband, so make sure the groupies know to stay away from you."

A gleam of satisfaction entered his eyes. "I'm glad we understand each other," he said. "And another thing—if Ricardo needs anything, you come to me. If you need anything, you come to me." His fingers spread out across her back, heating her skin through the material of the dress. "If we're both staying away from groupies and deacons, what do we do in the meantime to satisfy our needs?"

He was calm and composed, while his touch wreaked havoc with her senses, dragging her under the tide of his sensual influence. She shouldn't—couldn't want him.

"I couldn't care less what you do." Any minute now, he would look down and see she was a liar, see the way her nipples strained against the soft cotton of her bodice. "Use your hand, for all I care."

"Hmm. Doesn't have the same appeal."

"Rafe," she warned. She tried to ease out of his embrace, but found her efforts thwarted by his brute strength. "All right, you've proven your point. You're stronger than me. You can let me go now."

"Maybe I'm not done proving my point, *ángel*," he drawled. The sensuous sound of his voice tugged at her heartstrings.

He lowered his head in one swift motion and took her mouth, startling and arousing her at the same time. He cradled the back of her head in his palm, and her anger dissipated like morning fog in the first rays of sunlight. Her fingers curled into his powerful arms as he bent her over his arm. Teasing teeth tugged the sensitive flesh of her lower lip until she could no longer bear it and wrapped her arms tightly around his neck to urge a fuller exploration.

His expert tongue delved between her lips, stroking the sensitive cavern of her mouth to elicit a moan of burgeoning desire from the back of her throat. The taste of him was intoxicating, flooding her taste buds with a flavor that far surpassed the memories she'd tucked away in the deep recesses of her mind.

When Rafael slipped his hand over the curve of her breast and shaped the soft flesh, a shudder coursed through her. In the back of her mind, she knew she should be stronger than this, but she'd always been weak for him. Nothing had changed.

"Let me suck your nipples," he murmured.

Not waiting for a response, he lowered the straps of her dress and pushed her plump, swollen breasts to sit over the top of the bodice. On a groan, he lowered his head and pulled one dark nipple into his mouth. She gasped, the sharp jolt of pleasure that rushed through her echoing between her legs. He shifted from one breast to the other, focused, licked, stroked with his thumb until her shallow breathing filled the air between them.

She should stop him, but she couldn't. She arched her body, anxious to get more. The escalating ache almost unbearable, her fingers trailed through the dark, silky hairs on his head.

Weakened from the sensual maneuvers of his mouth, Rebekah let her head loll back.

The tip of his tongue traced the column of her throat and left a trail of moist heat in its wake. When he reclaimed her lips, she could do nothing but kiss him back and take the pleasure he offered. He kissed her long, hard, and thoroughly, holding her tight, crushing her bare breasts against his chest.

Her sensitive nipples rubbed against his white polo shirt while his large hands smoothed down her back and molded the curves of her hips and buttocks, heightening the sexual demands of her body.

When he lifted his mouth from hers, her quickened breath skated across her tingling lips as he watched her from his superior height. In the intimacy of the moment, she felt bare and vulnerable.

His blazing gaze locked with hers. "From now on, those nipples belong to me, and I'm the only one who gets to suck them." She trembled, aching from the raw sexuality of his words. "Anything you need," he reiterated, his accent thicker now, his sculpted lips just inches away, his voice raspy from the same hunger that coursed through her veins, "you come to me. *Anything.*"

She didn't miss the innuendo, nor did she miss the excited leap of her heart. His touch and his words made her wish for, want, need what she'd lived without for years. *Him.* All of him.

It scared her. He had been her world. She had abandoned her family for him.

She pushed away from him and he released her. She staggered back and braced her hand against the counter. Her body ached to be filled in the same way he had filled her mouth.

After righting her dress, she met his gaze when she could speak. "This doesn't mean anything," she said past swollen, quivering lips.

"You can deny it, but there's still something between us." The husky velvet tones of his voice moistened her already damp panties even more.

"There was always something between us, but it wasn't enough." There was no point in denying the message her body conveyed loud and clear. Her swollen nipples were still achy and clamored to get back into his mouth. "We can't go back, and sleeping with each other is *not* the answer."

"It's not the answer to our past problems, but it might help us get through the coming months during the divorce."

His suggestion was ridiculous. How could they have sex while trying to iron out a divorce? Sex would muddy the waters and cloud their judgment—hers, at least.

"What you're suggesting is not a good idea."

His gaze dipped to the front of her dress, surveying the proof of the passion that still existed between them. His lingering gaze had the same effect as a caress. Her nipples tightened in longing.

"I think you should leave." The whispered words were a struggle to get out. She needed to regroup.

"You should think about it, *mi ángel*." He trailed a finger down her cheek.

Rebekah turned away from his touch. "Go. Please."

She had to get him out of there. The maelstrom of feelings swirling through her could not be analyzed in her current state.

At first, she thought Rafael wouldn't leave. He remained standing just within reach, watching her, the heat from their fervent caresses weighing heavy on the air. Then, without another word, he left the kitchen.

She followed him into the foyer.

"Rafe." He glanced back, his hand on the doorknob. "You know it's over between us, don't you? This was just a slip up. There's no chance of anything happening between us again. Ever."

His enigmatic expression didn't change. "Good night, Rebekah."

She stared at the closed door. The reverberations of her heart shook her entire body. She touched a finger to her tingling lips.

Had those words been meant to convince him, or her?

CHAPTER 8

*R*icardo jumped up from the chair at the kitchen table and dropped his cereal bowl in the sink. He bolted from the kitchen before the doorbell could ring a second time. Rebekah picked up her purse and walked with a more leisurely pace toward the front door.

"*Buenos días, mijo,*" Rafael said, smiling down at his son.

"*Buenos días,*" Ricardo returned.

"I'll see you later," Rebekah said, reaching down to drop a kiss on her son's cheek and receive one from him in return.

She was on her way to the attorney's office, and they were on their way to the barber. Since Ricardo had asked, first thing this morning, to have Rafael take him for a haircut—no doubt prompted by the sight of his father's closely cropped hair—she had called his father to see if he could take Ricardo to the barber while she went to her appointment and ran other errands.

"Red looks good on you," Rafael commented. His gaze rested at the V-neckline just above the top button of her silk blouse.

"*Every* color looks good on Mom."

"I think you're right," Rafael said.

Heat suffused her cheeks. "Thank you, sweetie."

She saw the amusement in Rafael's eyes. He was having a good time with her discomfort. She had tossed and turned most of the night, dwelling on his kisses and the strokings of his tongue across her breasts. She had considered taking a cold shower, but at some point, exhaustion had taken over, and she awoke when Ricardo came into her room this morning. At least there were no telltale bags under her eyes.

"I'll be back by four," she said to Rafael.

"We'll be back soon after," he promised.

The three of them exited the house.

* * *

THE LAW OFFICE OF BUCHANAN, Rothstein, and Hoyt, located in the trendy, commercial district of Midtown, was decorated in muted tones of off-white and gray. Attorney Sterling Buchanan was fifteen minutes late for their meeting. Glancing at her watch, Rebekah hoped he hadn't forgotten their last minute appointment.

Just as the thought crossed her mind, she heard his deep voice.

"Bekah," he said, referring to her by the nickname he'd heard her older brother call her. "Sorry I'm late." He walked over, and when she stood up, he gave her a hug. "How've you been?"

He smiled down at her fondly. Handsome, with light mocha skin, a goatee, and mesmerizing eyes, Sterling was a dream. It was no wonder she'd had a crush on him from the age of twelve until she met Rafael.

"I've been better," Rebekah admitted.

Sterling ushered her into his office and waved her into one of the guest chairs. Once seated behind his large desk, he said, "Tell me what's going on."

Rebekah provided a detailed history of her marriage and everything she knew about the botched divorce. When she finished, she posed the question uppermost in her mind. "How long will it take to get the divorce?"

Sterling tapped his forefinger on his desk calendar. "It's hard to say. An uncontested divorce would take about two months. Your situation is complicated by a couple of factors that could draw out the length of the proceedings."

"What factors are those?" Rebekah asked with a sinking feeling.

"Ricardo, for one. Whenever there's a child involved, it complicates matters. Custody and visitation will have to be worked out. Then there's the issue of assets. Your husband's a wealthy man."

She nodded. "Yes, I know, but I don't want anything from him. Not for me, anyway. I'm sure Rafe will want to provide for Ricky, though."

Sterling shrugged. "Still, your husband is a California resident and you're a resident of Georgia. The first order of business is to get him to sign a waiver of jurisdiction so the divorce can be handled here. That shouldn't be a problem. His attorney will advise him it's preferable to handling the case in California. He stands to lose a lot more if they do."

"What's next?"

"I'll get in touch with his attorney. By the way, this is on the house." He smiled.

"No, I can't ask you to do that. I can pay you."

"Adam's practically a brother, so by extension, you're my sister, too. I know this is a tough situation you're in."

Rebekah sighed. "Thanks. I can't believe something like this could happen."

"You'd be surprised how often it does." Rebekah's eyebrows raised. "It's true. Courts screw up all the time. Clerks make mistakes, especially when they're overwhelmed. Judges sometimes don't sign documents in a timely fashion, which means we have to redo filings we've already made. Our paralegals spend a lot of time doing follow up. You should go sit in at Superior Court some time and watch the chaos." A pained expression came over his face.

"I'll take your word for it." Rebekah slung her purse over her shoulder. "Are you sure about doing this at no charge?"

"I'm sure. If the two of you want to end this marriage and can come to an agreement about Ricardo, I don't see a problem. I just need his attorney's name to get the ball rolling, and everything will be wrapped up before you know it."

* * *

As Rebekah drove her car under the carport, Rafael's SUV pulled into the driveway. Her son ran up to her when she got out of the car.

"Mom, how do I look?"

It was amazing how much Ricardo looked like his father with the new haircut. When Rafael walked up behind him, the resemblance was astounding. Gray eyes, high cheekbones, and a broad forehead figured prominently in the similarities.

"Very handsome." Rebekah touched his cheek and he grinned broadly up at her.

"Check this out." He lifted a handheld video game toward her. "Dad bought it for me. Can I show it to my friends?"

"Neat," she said, having no clue what she was looking at. "Yes, you can go show your friends your new toy."

"Cool!" She watched him run across the street in the cul-de-sac and knock on the door. Her neighbor answered and waved at her before letting Ricardo in.

"He has a lot of energy," Rafael remarked.

"Did you find it hard to keep up?"

Their eyes met and his piercing gaze held hers. "Not at all. I have a lot of energy too."

Awareness sizzled between them at the deliberate words.

Rebekah cleared her throat. "Well, thank you for taking him to the barber for me." She turned to go.

At the front door, his deep voice sounded close behind her. "Mind if I come in for a few minutes?"

Rebekah whirled in his direction. She thought she'd left him in the driveway. "I...don't think—"

"I'll only come in for a few minutes."

Last night made her realize she treaded on dangerous ground with Rafael. His proximity made her very aware of the height of his frame, the breadth of his shoulders, and each sinewy piece of bronze muscle she could see.

"Would you prefer to talk out here?" he asked when she didn't respond.

"No, I—" She could handle him. She had self-control. He no longer had the power to make her forego common sense and act on impulse. After her silent pep talk, she said, "No. Come in."

Inside, she dropped her purse on the foyer table. "Would you like something to drink?" she asked over her shoulder, making her way toward the kitchen. It was a strain to keep her voice normal.

"No, I'm fine. How did your meeting with the attorney go?"

Rebekah poured herself a glass of water and took several swallows before placing the glass on the table. "It went well. He plans to contact your attorney soon."

His eyes roamed over her exposed skin in the sleeveless blouse. Goose bumps sprang up and down the length of her arms. "Are you okay? You seem a little tense."

Yes, she was tense, and it was his fault. "I'm fine."

A sound from the foyer caught their attention. Ricardo and two of his friends traipsed into the kitchen.

"Wow, it's true," one of the boys said, staring up at Rafael in awe.

Rafael took the boy's hand and shook it. "Nice to meet you," he said with a smile.

"See, I told you!" Ricardo said. "He's my dad." He turned to Rebekah. "Mom, can I sleep next door tonight? We want to play video games."

Still flustered, it took a moment for Rebekah to answer. She turned to the other two boys. "Is it okay with your mother?"

Both heads bobbed in unison. "Yes, Miss Jamison. My mom sent me over to get your permission."

"If it's all right with her, it's all right with me."

"Yes!" The three boys ran upstairs, but not before one last backward glance at Rafael by one of Ricardo's young friends.

"I'll be right back," Rebekah said, following the boys. It only took a few minutes for her to make sure Ricardo had everything he needed for his night at the neighbor's. When he was safely back across the street, she rejoined Rafael in the kitchen.

Alone in the house with Rafael, Rebekah's pulse hammered a warning, alerting her she was at a disadvantage.

"Was there anything else you wanted to ask me?"

"We were discussing how tense you were." His voice was dangerously low and inviting.

"And I told you, I'm not tense. I'm fine."

"Turn around." The words conjured erotic images of him behind her. Her body moistened at the thought of doing what he asked and lifting her bottom against his hips. "Let me give you a massage."

"Oh." The erotic image dissipated. "*I'm fine.* Really."

"You used to like my massages." His voice lowered even more.

Magic hands, she used to call him. Once he'd eased the tension in her shoulders and back, he would ease the aching in her loins with firm, sure strokes.

"Relax," he said, taking matters into his own hands and turning her around so she faced the table. His long fingers began to move in a soothing motion across the knotted muscles. "You're really tense, *amada*."

66

The initial touch of his hands sent jolts of electricity darting across her skin. Despite his size and strength, his fingers moved gently across her shoulder blades, kneading the tight tissue with the skill of a professional masseur. Having been an athlete for years, he'd mastered the technique of manipulating the various muscles. He applied the right amount of pressure, and her eyes drifted closed. She had no choice but to let go and soften to his touch.

"That's better," he whispered.

The warmth exuding from him caressed her skin, making the back of her neck tingle. The slow ascension of arousal began somewhere deep inside her and climbed at a steady pace through her body.

He abandoned her shoulder to encircle one wrist and brought the back of her hand to his lips. Her eyes flew open.

The other hand slid down the length of the A-line skirt, smoothing over the roundness of her hip. She heard him take a deep breath. "Now I remember." His voice rumbled close to her ear. "Pomegranate Orchard is the name of the scent you wear."

"Rafe, I've already warned you." She retrieved her hand with a firm twist. A pulsing awareness thrummed through her, making her breathless and needy, wanting him with every fiber of her being. She turned to face him.

Bracing a hand on either side of her, he trapped her between him and the round table. "I'm not good at following directions."

"Keep your hands to yourself."

"You didn't mind a moment ago."

"I mean it." She didn't sound as harsh as she wanted to.

A crooked, unconcerned smile appeared on his face. "Well, if you don't want my hands on you," he said, "maybe my mouth is more to your liking."

The husky words invited her to bliss. Rafael dipped his head and slid his mouth across hers with little pressure. The gentle exploration gave her the option to pull away if she wanted to do so.

The moment his lips touched hers, she was lost, caught up in a tornado of desire that whisked its way through her. Hunger stirred to full life in her body, making her long for his hands and more intimate contact. Of their own volition, her palms slid across the contours of his broad chest and came to rest on his shoulders.

But he didn't touch her.

Slipping her arms around his neck, she drew him closer and opened her mouth beneath his to deepen the kiss, entwining her tongue with his.

Still, he didn't touch her.

She stroked her fingers across the short hairs at the nape of his neck and pressed her aching breasts against his chest. The nipples swelled and hardened on contact. With her full length against him, she could feel every inch of his hard body, breathe in his unique male scent. The hard ridge of his erection aroused her further, making her lift her leg to wrap her foot around his calf, and get up on tip toe to try to center it where she ached the most.

Finally, he touched her.

With a suddenness that took her breath away, he grabbed two handfuls of her bottom and lifted her until he was cradled in the valley of her thighs. Moisture filled her panties as she ground her hips against him.

"I see you've changed your mind," Rafael said, his voice rough with passion.

Without giving Rebekah a chance to answer, he spun her around so she faced away from him. She assumed the position, her fingers splayed out on top of the cool, wooden tabletop. She stood frozen, except for the trembling of her inner thighs, awaiting his next move.

His long fingers swept her thick hair aside to hang over her shoulder so he could drop tender kisses along her neck and the sensitive skin behind her ear. She closed her eyes to savor each connection of his lips to her flesh.

Before she could process his actions, his hands climbed up the back of her bare thighs. Heady desire engulfed her, weakening her resistance. Rendered helpless against the onslaught of his skilled touch, she longed to have him stroke her intimately, to ease the throbbing that blossomed between her legs.

"You won't be needing this," he said.

Not a second later, she heard the sound of tearing material and felt his hands on her naked hips. He'd torn off her panties! The fragile silk proved no match for the strength of his powerful hands. As he caressed her bare bottom, she fell onto her forearms, using the table to stay upright because her weakened knees could no longer support her.

"Rafe," she breathed.

Her senses reeled with an indecent swell of anticipation as her mind registered he was on his knees behind her. The folds of her skirt were bunched in his meaty fist while his mouth—his wicked, thorough mouth—pressed reverential kisses along the base of her spine. Lips parted, back arched, she squeezed her eyes tight as he showered kisses down the curve of her backside and licked the underside of her right cheek before his tongue lingered to flick a circular pattern around the flat mole of the left one.

With one hand, he nudged her legs wider. A low whimper escaped her throat. Her body pulsed, wanting what was on offer, consumed with need. And then...contact. The moist swirl of his tongue against her damp, aroused flesh was more than she could bear. With a helpless moan, her shaky knees gave way. The sureness of his hands eased her crumble to the floor.

She offered no resistance when he positioned himself between her open legs, leaving the path clear for the descent of his mouth. Her heart beat crazily in her chest in response to the gradual slide of his palms up the silky length of her thighs.

A guttural sound emerged from Rafael's throat, and he lowered his face between her legs, kissing her intimately. She slid backward on the cold tile, trying but not really wanting to escape his mouth, but he used his superior strength to hold her in place. He raised his head long enough to loop her right leg over his shoulder, licked at the sensitive flesh of her inner thigh, then directed his undivided attention to her moist center.

His grip tightened on her quivering thighs, keeping her open to every swipe of his rapacious tongue. She twisted against him, aching, throbbing, her breath harsh and shallow. His teeth gently nipped at her, teasing her sensitive skin for long seconds, leaving her gasping and forcing a long, low moan from her lips. She drowned in the pleasure of his mouth, her body growing wetter at the contented groans she heard from him, as if he enjoyed what he was doing as much as she enjoyed having him do it.

His tongue stroked the bundle of nerves with precision, then drew it between his soft lips with a prolonged suck. The single act catapulted her into the abyss. She exploded into his mouth. Her breasts thrust toward the ceiling with a sudden jerk while a hoarse cry of satisfaction tore from her lips as her body convulsed. She was out of control, shattering into a million pieces, lost in the sensations of an orgasm that fired through her with such force she couldn't catch her breath.

Even after her climax, his head remained between her legs. His mouth wrung every last quiver from her pulsing body, his actions akin to those of a starved man who aimed to capture every morsel and lick his plate clean.

When he finally leaned back on his haunches, he cleansed the sheen of her body's moisture from his lips with a swipe of his tongue. Hunger swirled in the depths of his eyes, darkening them to charcoal gray. He had been deprived of the release granted to her, and the massive bulge between his legs confirmed it.

Rebekah looked away from him as aftershocks vibrated through her. With trembling fingers, she pushed her skirt back down to her knees.

CHAPTER 9

*R*afael pushed up from the floor and helped Rebekah to her feet.

"I guess you're proud of yourself," she said, straightening her clothes. In the aftermath, she was angry. She hadn't handled him at all. He'd been in control the entire time. Two nights in a row she'd been like softened clay in his hands, unable to resist him.

"Actually, that's the last thing I have on my mind. I'm very horny right now." His admission didn't surprise her because of the blatant evidence. The old Rafael would have taken her on the floor, which made her wonder what had made him stop.

"Well, don't think I'll return the favor."

His dimples appeared and his eyes became alight with amusement. "Oh, I already know you don't like to do that—unless things have changed?"

"Nothing's changed." Feeling self-conscious, Rebekah combed her fingers through her voluminous hair. "And it's not that I didn't like to do it, it's that you wanted me to—to—"

"To let me finish in your mouth?"

Heat warmed her cheeks. "Yes." She reached up to close a

button that had popped open from her wanton writhing on the floor.

His hooded gaze remained on the movement of her fingers as they fumbled with the button. The exquisite orgasm he'd gifted her with made her bones feel like liquid and her skin hypersensitive. What happened between them couldn't be helped, she reasoned. His lovemaking skills hadn't diminished one iota in the intervening years. What woman could resist such an erotic onslaught?

"That's every man's fantasy," he said with a silky drawl.

"I'm sure..." She almost said she was sure he'd had plenty of women willing to do that for him, but she didn't. They had an agreement not to bring up the past anymore. "I'm sure it is."

Just behind Rafael she caught sight of the torn remains of black silk he had tossed behind him. He followed her line of vision and reached down to pick up the torn panties. When she reached out her hand to take it, he tucked it into the pocket of his jeans.

"What do you think you're doing?" she whispered fiercely, as if someone else stood in the kitchen with them.

"What does it look like I'm doing?" He headed toward the front door.

"You can't keep that. Give it to me!"

He ignored her, never faltering in his steps.

"Rafe!" He turned to face her just inside the door.

"Think about it," Rafael said.

"Think about what?"

"About us," he answered. "We both have needs, we're both adults, and we're still married. There's nothing wrong with us satisfying our needs with each other during the interim."

He made it sound so simple, but it would only complicate matters between them, and she had to consider the ramifications of her actions. Could she explore a purely sexual relationship with him and walk away unscathed at the end of it?

"It's a ridiculous idea," Rebekah said.

"Is it?" He pulled the underwear from his pocket and dangled it in front of her.

"You're a pig."

"Think about it."

She made a grab for her underwear, but he snatched it out of her reach.

One finger curled into the waistband of her skirt and drew her close. He dipped his head and pressed a quick kiss to her mouth. "It's not a crazy idea." His warm breath fanned across her lips. She gazed into his eyes, on the brink of abandoning her resolve and yielding to more ecstasy in his arms.

He released her, allowing his hand to drag along her buttocks. She took two steps backward and broke the spell.

His sensuous lips curved into a smile. *"Buenas noches, amada."*

Rebekah closed the door with a firm thump and pressed her back against it. She closed her eyes, unsuccessfully trying to will her breathing to return to normal. Her entire body shook. How could she have allowed herself to get so carried away? How could she have allowed him to stoke the flames inside her and reawaken her body to intimacies that made her long for him again?

It had taken several years to put her splintered heart back together after the tabloid story. The joy of becoming a mother had helped her through the pain, but the fear of getting hurt had caused her to delay involvement with anyone else for a long time. She had devoted her time to her son, working, and going to school to get her degree.

Rebekah groaned inwardly, pressing her palms to her heated cheeks.

"Enough, Rebekah," she whispered. "Get over it. He's only a man." A virile, sexy man who'd had her moaning his name and crying out *on the kitchen floor.*

She reminded herself he'd destroyed their marriage with his

selfish pursuits and caused her great humiliation. Because of him, she'd been forced to concede her parents had been right and had given her sound advice, which, to the detriment of her heart, she had disregarded in youthful ignorance.

Yet despite the mental catalog of reasons why she shouldn't want Rafael, her body couldn't connect the dots.

Letting out a slow breath through her lips, Rebekah pushed away from the door to go upstairs. She could not avoid a long, cold shower tonight.

* * *

BACK AT THE HOTEL, Rafael paced the floor slowly, deep in thought. The CNN newscaster gave an update on strife in other parts of the world, but he didn't hear a word the man said.

He swirled the amber liquid of his favorite bourbon before swallowing a mouthful of it.

He was so aroused he might have to soak in a tub filled with ice. His inadequate memory had in no way prepared him for the pleasure he'd received tonight. His body wanted inside hers with such ferocity it shook him. It had taken monumental restraint to rise from the floor instead of unzipping his pants and filling her with his hard length.

Despite her enthusiastic response, with one small, sane part of his brain, he'd recognized it was too soon, and she wouldn't handle that level of intimacy well. He'd set aside his own needs, but he doubted he'd be able to exercise the same level of restraint if he found himself in a similar circumstance again.

He came to a halt and drained his glass. His eyes remained on the view beyond the patio door. Long, rectangular buildings were covered in tiny squares of light in the darkness of night.

The thoughts that had speared through his mind earlier resurfaced. How would he manage the long separations for months at a time from his son? Another thought emerged. How would he manage the separation from his wife?

The seeds of an idea sprouted in his mind.

By some odd twist of fate, he and Rebekah were still married. What if they stayed married? What if he could convince her becoming a family was the best thing for Ricardo?

She didn't trust him because of the past, so it would take some convincing. He'd wooed her once, and maybe he could do it again. It would be hard, but he would have to back off, give her room, and let her feel comfortable.

With renewed purpose, he picked up his cell phone and punched in the number for his assistant.

It was time to head home, and he was taking his wife and son with him.

CHAPTER 10

*R*ebekah stroked her fingers down the strands of her ponytail, amazed she was on her way to California. She still didn't know how she'd managed to pack for the summer and wrap up her personal life in four days.

She stretched her legs, enjoying the roominess of the first class seat. Across the aisle, Ricardo sat next to the window with Rafael seated beside him. Their dark heads were huddled together over the video game Ricardo had hardly put down since his father purchased it.

Rafael looked formidable in a black shirt and black jeans that hugged his muscular frame. His deep voice floated across the aisle to her as he whispered to his son, stirring her emotions.

Her eyes lowered to the words of the e-reader in her hand, but no matter how she tried not to think about what Rafael had done to her and made her feel, she couldn't suppress the thoughts of their interlude in the kitchen. Every time he came to the house to see Ricardo, feelings of desire awoke and simmered beneath the surface.

She denied to herself that she looked forward to his visits with Ricardo, but each time the doorbell rang, her leaping heart betrayed the same excitement her son openly expressed. Fear she wouldn't be able to resist him in California filled her. Yet oddly, he hadn't done anything since that evening to make her feel he still wanted her.

He never again suggested they have what would amount to a sexual relationship to satisfy their mutual needs. In fact, he didn't even appear interested anymore, which conversely increased her attraction to the idea, despite her reservations.

How could she even contemplate such a thing? To make love with Rafael meant she would be at the mercy of her feelings. She'd already reluctantly acknowledged she couldn't become intimate with him without risking her heart in the process. Not when she knew at the end of a couple of months they would be divorced and living on opposite ends of the country.

The disturbing thoughts whorled around and around in her head like a circling bird of prey. She turned off the e-reader, leaned her head back, and closed her eyes.

Not for the first time, she wished he'd never touched her.

* * *

WHEN THEY LANDED at Los Angeles International Airport, as planned, Rafael walked ahead of Rebekah and Ricardo. She watched as he fielded questions from the photographers who encircled him as soon as they recognized him. With Ricardo's hand tucked securely in hers, she walked swiftly past as if she didn't know him. His personal assistant, Lydia, approached and hustled them into a waiting limo.

Ricardo's eyes opened wide. "I've never been in a limo before," he whispered in awe.

"Lucky you." Lydia grinned. Her dark eyes crinkled at the corners behind black-framed glasses. "I didn't ride in a limo until my high school prom at seventeen years old." With her slender body and blue and black shoulder length hair, she barely looked more than seventeen at the moment, though Rebekah knew she was in her early thirties.

"Is it always so crazy for him?" she asked, referring to Rafael.

Her eyes drifted to Ricardo, who knelt on the leather seat and peered through the tinted windows at the passersby. Her unease grew tenfold when she thought about his safety and how the media exposure could affect him.

"Not always," Lydia replied. "Sometimes one or two fans will approach him for an autograph, but if he's lucky, no one will bother him and he can sail through." She shrugged. "Then other times, you get the circus like today."

A few minutes later, their luggage was in the trunk and Rafael slid onto the seat. Lydia tapped the glass partition separating them from the driver, and they pulled away from the curb.

Rafael rested his arm against the back of the seat and turned to Rebekah. His fingers lightly touched her ponytail. He hadn't touched her since the night in the kitchen. The warmth in his gaze heated her blood and tripled her pulse.

"We're on our way home," he said.

"I can't wait to see *your* house."

He only smiled at her.

The intensity in Rafael's eyes caused a thread of fear to run down her spine. On his turf now, the constant interaction would erode any emotional barriers she tried to erect against him. The battle of wills had begun.

She knew two things about her husband. He loved a good fight. And he never lost.

* * *

INSTEAD OF GOING STRAIGHT to the house, they took a detour and went west on I-10 toward the Santa Monica Pier.

Ricardo's eyes lit up when he saw the Pacific Ocean.

Pointing through the window to the pier, he said, "Mom, look! There's a Ferris wheel."

"An entire amusement park is located there, and an aquarium," Rafael added.

"Are we coming to this beach?" Ricardo asked.

Rafael nodded, giving his son an indulgent smile. "Yes. This is where we'll build the sand castles."

"Can we stay the whole day?"

"Sure can."

"Yes!" When they pulled away, Ricardo craned his neck to keep the pier in sight. "I can't wait."

On Highway 10, they went north. Since she'd never been to California before, Rebekah felt some of her son's excitement when she recognized the community names of Brentwood and Bel Air.

Before long, they arrived at Rafael's residence in the affluent neighborhood of the Hollywood Hills. They pulled into the gated compound, and the closing gate shut out the rest of the world.

Though not a mansion, the house was a far cry from the motel room they used to rent on a weekly basis ten years ago. They stopped at the end of the driveway in front of the sprawling four-bedroom and four and a half bath ranch house. A lush, green lawn and pebble gardens gave the impression of having landed at an oasis.

"Wow," Rebekah murmured under her breath when they entered the house. She stared up at the vaulted ceilings and open rafters of the living room. She recognized Mexican paintings and sculptures in the tastefully decorated room of large furniture and earth tones.

A signal from Lydia prompted Rafael to look at his watch. He grimaced. "Make yourselves at home and take a tour of the house. I need to make an important call in my office in the back. It shouldn't take long."

When he disappeared, Ricardo looked up at his mother. "You heard your dad," she told him. "Let's check this place out!"

With Ricardo leading the way, they walked into the media room where a lowered screen hung from the ceiling. A wet bar and plenty of seating for guests made Rebekah wonder if Rafael entertained often. Both rooms boasted large windows and offered breathtaking views of the Los Angeles area and the canyon below.

On the back side of the house was a small brick building, which Rebekah guessed was Rafael's office. There was a hot tub, and blue-green water filled the oval swimming pool, which was afforded sufficient privacy by the trees and bushes around the perimeter of the yard. From the back yard, they stepped into the modern, black-and-white kitchen with charcoal tile. Dropped ceiling lights hung over the counters flanking the sink.

Rafael found them in the master bedroom.

"You *were* quick," Rebekah remarked.

"Fortunately. I needed to discuss some changes in a contract we're in the middle of negotiating." His eyes found hers. "Well, what do you think?"

The master bedroom was just as tastefully decorated as the rest of the house. The oversized king bed in the middle of the room faced a large window that looked out onto another view of Los Angeles. Deep blue dominated the decor. Two small couches with blue and green pillows in the sitting area sat on opposite sides of a massive coffee table with magazines stacked on top of it. There was a spalike bathroom, a white fireplace, built-in bookshelves, a wet bar with several bottles of liquor, and a refrigerator in a corner gave the impression of a self-contained room.

"You have a beautiful home, Rafael. You've done very well for yourself."

His body had taken beatings for years, but it had paid off. The young man from Mexico City had become a millionaire who lived among celebrities in the privacy of the Hollywood Hills. Although she never approved of his line of work, Rebekah was proud of him.

"I like it," Ricardo piped up.

Rafael switched his attention to his son. "You do? Have you seen your room yet?"

Ricardo shook his head.

"*Vamonos.*"

Rebekah followed behind, her stomach twisting at the strong relationship already developed between them. The separation would be difficult when the end of the summer came and they returned to Georgia.

CHAPTER 11

For the next couple of days, Rafael remained preoccupied filming new commercials for the chain of gyms that had licensed his name. During the interim, he dispatched his assistant to help Rebekah and Ricardo get acclimated to their new environs. She drove them around, showing Rebekah places where she could go shopping, the best restaurants, and pointed out some of the tourist attractions she could return to on her own.

On Saturday afternoon, after the final taping, Rafael pulled his late model Range Rover into the garage and parked next to the Lexus sedan he'd left for Rebekah's use. She had told him the night before she and Ricardo would venture out alone and go to the Santa Monica Pier, so he was surprised to see the car in the garage.

He entered the house and walked into the kitchen, and he stood for a moment at the French doors. Through the glass, he could see Rebekah and Ricardo in the pool. He eased open the door and stepped out.

She wore a purple, one-piece bathing suit tied around her neck, but because of the immediate tightening in his loins at her appearance, it might as well have been a string bikini. The water glimmered on her dark skin, and the suit lifted her breasts and showed off the curve in her waist and the flair of her hips. Her long, dark hair was plastered to her back, and he watched as she brushed a loose tendril from her face.

She frolicked and played with their son, splashing water on him, and tossing around a brightly colored inflated ball. Her throaty laughter and his squeals of delight filled the back yard.

"Okay, sweetie, I'm tired. Let me take a break."

"Dad!"

Rafael smiled. "Looks like you two are having fun."

"Mom's tired. Are you coming in, Dad?"

Rafael's gaze traveled behind his son to Rebekah. "Yes, I will," he said.

* * *

WHEN RAFAEL RETURNED, Rebekah was seated in one of the chairs around the pool. The sight of his long, well-muscled legs in a pair of dark swim trunks made her abdominal muscles clench in reaction. Her eyes remained riveted to his masculine form until she realized he had spoken.

He gave her a questioning look. "I said, I thought you were going to the Santa Monica Pier today."

Rebekah blinked, clearing her throat before she answered. "He didn't want to go without you," she explained.

"Are you going back into the pool?"

"I'm tired. It's your turn. Have fun."

Rafael nodded. Then he took off running alongside the pool. "Incoming!" he yelled, and did a cannonball into the deep end.

Ricardo clapped and held up his arms in the sign of a touchdown. "I wanna try!"

Rebekah sat forward in her chair. "Ricky, I don't think that's a good idea, sweetie."

"He'll be fine. I'm right here. Go ahead, *mijo*. Let me see what you've got."

Rebekah remained perched on the edge of her chair until Ricardo was safely lifted into his father's arms after landing in the pool with a much smaller splash.

"*Bien hecho!*"

She watched father and son laugh together, Ricardo's little arms wrapped around Rafael's wide neck.

"I wanna go again," she heard her son say in a loud whisper.

Rafael boosted him out of the water, and Ricardo repeated his actions. Two more times he got a running start and jumped into the water near Rafael. Convinced she had overreacted, Rebekah sat back to watch their interaction. On the fourth try, though, Ricardo missed his footing and went crashing down on his hands and knees on the hard concrete.

Rebekah shot out of the chair not one second after he hit the ground. Without looking at her, Rafael lifted his hand to forestall her rush to Ricardo. He waded over to where Ricardo remained on the ground.

"Get up, let me see," he said. His voice held none of the cooing warmth she would have used with Ricardo after such a nasty spill.

She stood there, with her hands on her hips, longing to rush over to him. It was difficult to watch him stand gingerly and edge over to his father, his brown face furrowed in a frown as he tried not to let the tears spill from his eyes.

Rafael lightly tapped Ricardo's skinned knee. "Looks fine to me. How do you feel?"

"Okay." His voice was soft and wobbly.

"Try it again, and this time, watch your step, understand?"

Ricardo nodded. "Yes, Dad."

His voice sounded stronger, but Rebekah felt as if her heart would explode in her chest. She watched, holding her breath as Ricardo took off running again. After two more successful cannonballs, he seemed back to normal, and both he and his father turned their attention to playing with the ball.

In order to survive the rest of the afternoon without having a heart attack as she watched them roughhousing in the water, Rebekah went into the house to shower and change clothes. By the time she finished and started dinner, they had left the pool.

She finished cooking while Rafael and Ricardo showered and dressed. Rafael cleaned Ricardo's scrapes with hydrogen peroxide, much to the boy's dismay, and placed an adhesive bandage on his skinned knee. Over dinner, they made plans to go to the beach on Sunday.

After the meal, Ricardo went to his room, and Rafael helped Rebekah clean up and put away the leftovers.

"Dinner was delicious. Thank you."

Rafael had a housekeeper who came only during the week and cleaned, cooked meals, and did laundry.

"You're welcome."

Rebekah turned the water on in the sink to wash the few dishes.

"I know you didn't approve of what I did with Ricardo today, but I'm glad you didn't interfere."

Rebekah took a deep breath filled with the clean, male scent of Rafael from his not too long ago shower. "It was difficult." She turned off the water and turned to face him. "Rafe, I know you're trying to make him tougher, but he's only eight years old. He's not a grown man."

"Not yet, but he will be, and the sooner his training starts, the better."

"Training?"

Ricardo rested his hands on the counter and stared out the window at the fading light. "He needs toughening up, Rebekah." He looked at her again. "He can't run and cry to his mommy every time he takes a fall. And you shouldn't be there to hold him every time he does."

"I've been taking care of him all this time, and he's turned out just fine. He's also had other male influences in his life—my brother Adam, and he spends a lot of time with my father."

"Your father?" He sounded skeptical. "Has your father ever run through a few punches with him?"

"You don't live in the streets of Mexico City. You live in the Hollywood Hills, for heaven's sake! I live in a suburb of Atlanta."

His gaze pinned her. "Do you have any idea what's going to happen when other kids find out who his father is? They're going to test him, challenge him, and make him prove he's strong and able to fight like me."

Rebekah had never thought about it before, but she realized Rafael may be right. Kids could be cruel. As a middle school teacher, she saw how the boys behaved, full of testosterone and the need to prove their manhood long before they entered it.

"He's only eight." Would they gang up on her baby?

"That's why we start now." His look softened. "I know you're worried, but he'll be fine. He needs to toughen up. If he doesn't, the other children will eat him alive. When he falls, he needs to get right back up and act as if nothing happened."

That's what Rafael had done. She'd been to very few of his underground fighting matches, unable to stomach the brutality of the sport. She'd seen it all—bruised ribs, a dislocated shoulder, fractures—nothing could keep him down. No matter how many kicks and punches were leveled at him, he kept on fighting.

In the ring, the adrenaline had kept him going, and she sensed he couldn't really feel the blows. Only later, once he was at home and she had to clean his cuts and bruises, and he soaked his sore muscles in a warm bath, did he show any indication the fighting took a toll.

"I'll teach him how to fall and how to tense his muscles to deflect the power of a punch. He won't start a fight, but he'll know how to stop one. There's a difference."

"Maybe you shouldn't have been such a good fighter," Rebekah joked with a weak smile.

"He would have to learn these things anyway, but I admit, having a pro wrestler as a father could be a negative."

"I guess it could be positive too," Rebekah said. "He could threaten to have you beat up the other kids. Or he could even throw out the 'my dad can beat up your dad' card."

Rafael chuckled and leaned against the marble counter. His eyes lit up as his handsome face transformed into lighthearted merriment. "I need to remember that and remind him he can use me to threaten the other kids whenever he needs to."

Rebekah laughed too, and she could feel herself falling, tumbling into long-buried feelings. What was she doing here living under the same roof with the man who should be her ex-husband, talking about how to raise Ricardo and...enjoying it?

Secretly, she'd missed seeing him the past few days while he shot the commercials. Would he spend more time with them now?

Rafael looked thoughtfully down at her. "Let's go out to dinner tomorrow night."

"Where did you have in mind? Ricky mentioned—"

"Without Ricardo. Just you and me." His gaze didn't waver, and his voice was different. The lowered bass rippled through her, heating her skin.

Her breath stalled for a moment. "Just the two of us?" She followed up her breathless question with another. "What will we do with Ricky?"

"I'll hire someone to watch him. My housekeeper may even be willing to babysit for the night. I'll hire a car, and we'll get dressed up and go somewhere nice."

Trying to appear nonchalant, although she was excited by the prospect of an evening out, Rebekah said, "Sounds like a good idea. It'll be nice to get out and see the city at night."

"Do you remember our first date?"

The change of subject surprised her. She nodded.

A wry smile lifted a corner of his mouth. "What a mess. I had left my wallet at my apartment, and I didn't have any money to cover the meal. You had to put it on the credit card your father gave you for emergencies."

She remembered it well. He'd been so embarrassed and upset. "You paid me back."

"My car broke down, and we had to walk part of the way until we could get to a phone, and I could call one of my friends to pick us up."

She had left her cell phone at home so her father couldn't reach her. She remembered the night in vivid detail. It was the night of their first kiss—and the night she had fallen in love with him.

She had felt safe with him as they walked the dark streets. He'd been a big man even then, though now he was more muscular after years of conditioning.

"It gave us time to talk, and you held my hand the entire way," she said.

He laughed dryly and shook his head.

Rebekah realized what she recollected as fond memories were not the same for him. His macho pride had taken a beating that night.

"None of that mattered to me," she said softly. "All I cared about was being with you."

"I know." He smiled down at her. "But now, I can afford the things I couldn't before. I can take care of you and Ricardo the way you deserve."

Rebekah shook her head. "I don't want a dime from you. My attorney understands how I feel. You don't owe me anything because you did this on your own. Just take care of Ricky."

"Not many women would feel that way, Rebekah. You do know I'm rich now, don't you?" He grinned, and the reappearance of his dimples made her heart race.

"I know."

He shifted and shoved his hands deep into his pockets.

"Tomorrow night, I'm going to spoil you."

"Rafe—"

"I want to."

She smiled. "Well…it just so happens I love to be spoiled."

"Good. I'll make the reservations."

Then, as if he didn't want to give her time to change her mind, he made his way out of the kitchen.

Rebekah slowly released her breath. Dinner with Rafael, alone. It would be the first time they would spend an extended period alone together since their arrival in California. Under normal circumstances, Ricardo was always nearby, and she and Rafael usually went their separate ways early in the evening.

Tomorrow night, for the first time, it would be just the two of them.

CHAPTER 12

*R*ebekah leaned toward the mirror in her bedroom to apply mascara and eyeliner. She had used a curling iron to add large curls to her hair and then pinned the thick tresses atop her head, making them look messy, yet neat at the same time. The black-and-white wraparound dress she wore was one of the few dresses she'd brought to California. With the addition of minimal jewelry and high-heeled sandals, she was ready for the evening out with Rafael.

She and Rafael had fallen into comfortable conversation earlier during the day, bantering back and forth with ease. The day they spent on the beach near the pier had been enjoyable and made them more relaxed around each other. Only once had there been cause for tension, and it had occurred when a fan wanted to take a photo of Rafael while he played with Ricardo. He told the man in no uncertain terms he did not have permission to take a picture of his son, and he made him wait until Ricardo moved out of the range of the shot.

Rebekah peeked in on Ricardo. The amber glow of the nightlight was enough for her to see he was comfortably under the covers, flat on his back, arms spread wide across the bed.

She quietly closed the door and walked toward the living room where she knew Rafael waited. They would soon be off for a late dinner in a private dining room at Spago Beverly Hills, the flagship restaurant of famed chef and restaurateur, Wolfgang Puck. Lydia would stay with Ricardo until their return.

Rafael wore a dark suit and stood in the living room looking out at the view. Their eyes met in the reflection in the wall of windows and he turned around.

"I'm ready," Rebekah said, smoothing damp palms over the material of her dress. She felt as if they were going on another first date.

Rafael's gaze flicked over her, but he didn't say a word. "Let's go then. The limo's waiting." He walked past her to open the front door, and the scent of sandalwood wafted up into her nostrils.

She swallowed back her disappointment when he didn't comment on her appearance, but her disappointment was short-lived. As they walked to the waiting car, his hand came to rest against the small of her back, filling her body with warmth and turning her lower limbs to jelly.

He leaned toward her, so close the light brush of his lips tickled her ear. "You look lovely tonight," he said in a low rumble. "I'm going to have to fight to keep other men away from you."

Rebekah smiled and cast him a coquettish look. "That won't be necessary," she said before slipping into the car. She crossed her legs, avoiding his smoldering gaze.

"Why is that?" His hand slid along the top of the leather seat and she felt him wrap a loose curl around his finger.

"You have to ask?" Their playful banter was escalating.

The driver closed the door, and Rafael leaned closer, his eyes glittering with interest in the dark interior. "Is it because you're all mine tonight?" he asked in a husky whisper.

Warmth crept into her cheeks. She swallowed as excitement swept through her. "Rafe—"

His fingers slipped from her hair and encircled the back of her neck, stemming the flow of words. The warmth of the contact of skin against skin surged down her torso and settled in her pelvis.

"We'll move as fast or as slow as you want, Rebekah, but we both know the outcome will be the same." His hooded gaze lowered to her lips. "It's inevitable, and there's nothing wrong with it."

"It's still a bad idea to sleep with each other to satisfy a biological need. As if—as if we're two people in the middle of an affair instead of a divorce."

"There are people who are divorced who still get together every now and again and have sex. Did you know that?" He said it as if he were educating her about a solution to a science equation.

"Did you know we're not those people? Those types of situations are usually dysfunctional." Despite her comments, she'd been seriously considering his suggestion.

His hand fell away and he straightened in the seat. "I don't think our situation will be dysfunctional," he said in a firm tone.

* * *

WHEN THEY ARRIVED at the restaurant, they entered through a side door, and one of the staff ushered them down a hallway toward the private dining room Rafael had reserved.

After the server took their order, Rebekah took a sip of water, her choice of beverage for the evening.

Her gaze roved around the dimly lit space painted in rich brown and a deep gold color. Their small table sat in the middle of a room large enough to accommodate several tables. One wall made of frosted glass provided privacy while, at the same time, allowing additional light to enter the room.

"Are you enjoying your stay in California so far?" Rafael asked.

Rebekah nodded. "Will your schedule be slowing down this week?"

"Yes. I want to spend more time with Ricardo. Before you know it, the summer will be over."

"He'll like that. He adores you."

He smiled, as if to himself. "I can't imagine my life without him. What was he like as a baby?"

Rebekah groaned. "Awful. I barely got any sleep the last couple of months before he was born. He moved around so much. It was as if he couldn't wait to get out!"

Rafael chuckled. "So he's been a bundle of energy since his time in the womb?"

"Definitely. Once he started walking, that was the end of my peace of mind. And he had an obsession with paper, so I had to keep my textbooks and homework up high so he couldn't tear them up. I would give him old magazines to tear apart instead." Rebekah noted the wistful look in Rafael's eyes. She swallowed. "You know, when he was a toddler, I tried to reach you one more time. But...well, your people wouldn't let me talk to you directly."

Rafael frowned. "The only *people* I had was Marty, and he would've told me if you'd called."

"I didn't speak to Marty. I spoke to that horrible woman who worked for him. She wouldn't let me speak to you or Marty, and she more or less told me I could take a number."

"*What?*"

"She..." Rebekah stared at him as a disgusting thought entered her mind. "Don't tell me—you were sleeping with her, weren't you?"

"I wasn't sleeping with her," he bit out.

"But that didn't stop her from seeing me as a threat." Rebekah lifted her hand to her mouth. "Oh my God," she said in a barely audible whisper.

"Don't, Rebekah."

"Really?" She shook her head in disgust. It had been so humiliating as she tried to get the woman to allow her to speak to Rafael. "I'm not allowed to get mad because some woman who had the hots for you wouldn't give you the message that you're the father of my child? Even if she didn't believe me, the bi—" Rebekah took a calming breath and fisted her hand on top of the table. "The woman could have at least told you just in case I was telling the truth—which I was."

"There were other ways to get in touch with me if you really wanted to. You could have hired a lawyer to gain access to me."

He made it sound so easy. He wasn't the one who'd had to beg for an audience. *I didn't want anything from you.*

Rafael sat back. His eyes flashed in anger. "Why would you when you could run home to your daddy? Our life didn't live up to your standards, so you went back to Atlanta the first chance you got and used my traveling as an excuse."

Rebekah's mouth fell open. "How dare you accuse me of something like that? I *did not* run home. I went to visit my parents. You were gone for weeks at a time."

"You could have come with me."

"I didn't want to."

"*Sí. Comprendo ahora.* It's always whatever Rebekah wants, right? You didn't want to come, so you didn't. You didn't want me to know you were pregnant, so I didn't. Ricardo is my son, and he and I should've known each other right from the beginning. I should have been lying next to you at night when you couldn't sleep."

"How exactly would that have worked?" Rebekah asked with saccharine sweetness. "We only had a full-size bed. Where were the other women going to sleep?"

Rafael slammed his large fist onto the table, and Rebekah jumped involuntarily. The sound was so loud she assumed the only reason the table hadn't broken apart was because he hadn't intended for it to.

"All right, here we go," the server said, smiling as she brought in their salads.

Rebekah turned her attention to the young woman, ignoring Rafael's glare from across the table.

After placing a plate in front of each of them, the server held up a pepper mill and asked, "Pepper?" They waved it away and she left them alone again.

"Look at us," Rebekah said. "We can't even have a civil conversation without Ricky as a buffer between us. We keep throwing up the past and we're hurting each other. He's the only good thing between us, and we need to focus on working together for his sake."

Rafael clenched his silverware. "We can't fix this, can we?"

"No, we can't." Rebekah distanced herself from thoughts of reconciliation. That wasn't what she wanted anyway, was it? "Why even talk about fixing anything? We can't go back in time and change our behavior. It's over, Rafe. It's been over. We were young and impulsive, and we made mistakes."

"So there's no point in trying again?" His voice was quiet. He watched her intently.

Rebekah looked down at her plate. "We have too much baggage—from each other. Even if we could try again, I don't want your life. I don't want people writing stories about me every time I go to the grocery store. I don't want my son photographed at school and afraid to play in the yard because paparazzi are hiding nearby trying to get a picture of him. What kind of life is that?" She sighed. "The life you're living is so different from us. How can you protect him when he's here with you in California?"

"The same way I've been doing since you arrived. There are

no guarantees, Rebekah, but you don't have to live in fear for his safety." He stabbed the vegetables on his plate with his fork. He stared down at his salad, and the heavy movement of his chest indicated he still struggled to calm down.

Their ruined meal was continued in silence. When the server returned with their dinner, she asked if the salads were okay because they were hardly touched. They assured her everything was fine, and she set the meals on the table and disappeared again after checking to make sure they didn't need anything else.

"Did you ever do drugs?" Rebekah asked.

"No. Despite what that article said, only a few of the wrestlers I knew did the hard-core stuff, but a lot of them popped painkillers like candy. They needed them to get past the pain of their injuries."

Rebekah pushed the chicken around on her plate. "Why did you quit?"

When he lifted his eyes, she was shocked by the sadness in their bleak depths. He thought for a moment before he answered.

"A few years ago, my wrestling contract was getting close to renewal. I was making a lot of money for the WWE. My action figures, T-shirts, pencils, everything sold well. Marty and I discussed a couple of options to get me more money. He planned to negotiate a salary increase for me and a greater percentage of the proceeds from the sales of merchandise with my image and name.

"Around the same time, there was this kid—well, not a kid, really. He was twenty-one or twenty-two, about the same age I was when I started in professional wrestling." He frowned, and she realized he wasn't really looking at her. His gaze looked *through* her. "I have to laugh sometimes when people say wrestling is fake. The blood is real, the punches are real, the body slams are real. It's choreographed, and we practice our moves to make sure we get them right, but there's nothing *fake* about what we do. The problem is, no matter how much you rehearse, mistakes still happen."

He swallowed, and Rebekah feared his next words. She stared at him, holding her breath, not daring to interrupt because she wanted to hear what he had to say as much as he needed to tell it.

"Poor Little Rich Kid was his stage name. He came from a wealthy family and didn't want to go into their business, so he went into wrestling instead." Rafael laughed shortly and shook his head in disbelief. "When he made his entrance, he would hand out one and five dollar bills to the audience. Rich was going to be a star, and we all knew it.

"One night, he and another wrestler were in the ring, giving a great performance. The other wrestler lifted Rich upside down to drop him on his head in a move called the Tombstone piledriver. The key is to keep your opponent's head above your knees, so when you drop to your knees, his head doesn't actually hit the mat. It didn't work that night. His hold on Rich slipped, and instead of his knees hitting the canvas mat first, Rich's head hit first. He broke his neck. Rich became permanently paralyzed from the neck down."

Rebekah gasped. She lost what little appetite she had left.

The sound caused Rafael to focus on her again. "Before that, I never seriously considered the danger of what I did. Because of what happened to Rich, I told Marty I wanted out and wouldn't renew my contract. He tried to convince me to stick it out a few more years, but once my contract ended, I retired."

* * *

THEY STRUGGLED through the rest of the evening, talking about mundane topics. They didn't argue again, but something had changed. Rebekah barely mustered any excitement when the restaurant owner, Wolfgang Puck, came in on one of his surprise visits to the restaurant to greet diners.

Later, she couldn't recall the taste of a single morsel of what she ate. As Rafael and Wolfgang chatted amicably, she thought about how many times he'd risked getting hurt in cage matches, flying off the top of the ring ropes, taking blows to his body with chairs, and who knew what else he'd done.

Compared to other popular wrestlers, his career had been a short one. Although relieved he was no longer fighting, nausea still settled in her stomach at what he must have gone through over the years. *He* could have been the victim in a botched maneuver. The thought terrified her so much her heart raced.

Rebekah couldn't ignore the meaning of the physical reaction she experienced at the thought of Rafael getting hurt. She took off the blinders and admitted the truth.

She was still in love with her husband.

CHAPTER 13

*B*ack at the house, Rebekah sat with her arms wrapped tightly around her knees in bed, staring at the painting on the opposite wall. She couldn't get the conversation with Rafael at Spago out of her mind.

Filled with guilt, she wanted to go to him and express her regret for not trying harder to get in touch with him and tell him about Ricardo. She wanted to tell him how sorry she was she hadn't been more supportive of his career choice.

Tears filled her eyes, and she squeezed them shut, pressing her face to her knees. She fought the urge to feel close to him, to make love to him. Desire flooded her veins, heightened by the thought of him getting hurt or permanently damaged.

In truth, she wanted a little bit of what she'd lost nine years ago. She wanted the pleasure and the passion, even if she didn't have his undying love. She needed to see him, touch him, hold him, but she was paralyzed by the fear of rejection. Would he forgive her angry words at dinner?

Would he care if she told him she still loved him?

* * *

RAFAEL HAD STRIPPED out of his shirt and jacket as soon as he could. He sat on the sofa in the sitting area of his bedroom, his bare feet crossed at the ankles and resting on top of the coffee table, clothed in only the trousers he'd worn to dinner.

The conversation at Spago made it clear he and Rebekah didn't have a chance of getting back together. By the end of dinner, she'd become distant, hardly saying a word, and she'd hardly touched her meal. Since the evening had deteriorated into unpleasantness, he'd canceled the other events he had planned for their night out.

Her father had been right to refuse him when he'd asked for her hand in marriage. She'd deserved better—not the pain and public humiliation he'd caused her. Because of him, she'd abandoned the safety and security of her family and had been forced to live in a cheap motel without all the comforts of a clean home and a loving family.

Their day at the pier had given him false hope and made him believe they might have a chance. Now he knew the truth. The thought of being separated from her and Ricardo at the end of the summer was agonizing, but he would have to accept the consequences of his actions.

Rafael ran his hand over his face and dropped it in a heavy thump on the table next to the sofa. With a grunt, he pushed himself up from the chair. He might as well go to bed.

As he moved across the carpet, a knock on the door sounded so lightly he almost didn't hear it.

"Come in."

Hesitantly, Rebekah entered the room. She'd let her hair down, and it fell onto her shoulders and down her back in loose curls. He watched as she closed the door by backing into it.

"I know I shouldn't be here," she whispered. She pulled her lower lip between her teeth.

He ran his gaze down the front of her thin white nightshirt and wished he hadn't. She was braless, the protrusion of her nipples prominently displayed. The hem of the shirt stopped several inches above her knees.

Dios! What was she doing in here barely dressed?

His shaft jumped, excited by her presence. Rafael swallowed, his throat as arid as desert sand. "What is it?" he asked harshly.

He clenched one fist, steeling himself against her involuntary flinch at his tone. Uncertainty hovered in her brown eyes, coupled with another emotion he couldn't read.

"I wanted to tell you I..." She stopped, seemed to think better of what she had been about to say, then continued. "I'm sorry I didn't tell you about Ricardo sooner. Because of me, you've missed out on so much of his life, and I hope you can forgive me."

"I've already—"

"I'm sorry I wasn't a better wife to you. When I went back to Atlanta to visit my parents, I didn't leave you, despite what you thought. I just needed to get away while you were out of town. I didn't work, and I didn't have any friends in Las Vegas. I was lonely without you because you were gone all the time. It was hard to attend your matches because I couldn't stand to see you get hit over and over again, sometimes watching you bleed. Especially in the beginning, when you were involved in underground fighting. Because even though you always won, you would be so badly bruised and swollen, it—" Her voice cracked and she glanced away for a moment to compose herself. "It tore me apart."

Now he understood what he saw in her eyes. Fear. His recounting of Rich's story must have made her imagine a similar accident happening to him.

"We both made mistakes. It's in the past." She nodded, but she still appeared disturbed by her thoughts. "I was always fine."

"You were, but I wasn't," she said softly.

The husky intonation of her voice made the hairs on the

back of his neck stand up. She was so close, so tempting, the craving inside him increased at a dramatic clip.

"If that's all, I think it's time for you to go back to your room. It's late," he said tersely, in a vain attempt to divert his desire for her.

Ever since he'd laid eyes on her back in Atlanta, making love to her had consumed his thoughts and increased after what happened between them in her kitchen. He could still taste her and hear her jagged breaths. The longer she stayed in this room, the harder the battle to repress the bone-deep hunger he held for her. If she didn't leave soon, he may not let her leave.

Rebekah laughed nervously. "If I didn't know any better, I'd think you were trying to get rid of me."

He didn't see the humor in the situation. "I am."

Startled, the smile on her face dissolved, only to be replaced by a pained expression. "I don't understand."

"*¿No entiendes?*" he growled in Spanish, because he was at the end of his rope, unable to think and function like normal. His shoulders, rigid with the need to maintain control, ached as if in a vice grip. "Then let me explain." He strode toward her. In a lowered voice, he spoke slowly so she could understand every word he said. "If you don't get out of here in the next three seconds, I can't promise you will ever be able to leave this room tonight. Because all I can think about is bending you over the arm of that sofa, or dragging you down onto the carpet, or laying you across those sheets. The position really doesn't matter, Rebekah, because they all end the same way—with me deep inside you."

Her lips parted on a silent gasp. Emotion flared to life in her eyes. "That's what I want."

The earth shifted under his feet. His hard flesh strained against the zipper of his trousers. "Rebekah—"

"I mean it." She stepped closer and ran her soft hands over

the contours of his chest. "I want to feel close to you, Rafe. I *need* to feel close to you."

He grasped her slender wrists in his hands, holding her fast. If this was a dream, he prayed he wouldn't wake up. "Are you sure?" He wanted to be unselfish and do the right thing—send her away so she wouldn't regret her actions in the morning, but she was making it so hard.

"*Yes.*"

The word was a seductive hiss. She rose up on her toes and pressed a soft kiss against the corner of his mouth, another to the column of his throat, drifting downward to lick the hammering pulse at his collarbone. A tremor of desire traveled through him. With one hand beneath her buttocks, he lifted her high. It took little effort, as he'd lifted men twice her size over his head. Flush against his chest, she wrapped her legs around his waist.

With a guttural groan of her name, he buried his fingers into the soft thickness of her hair, claiming her mouth, filling it with the probe of his tongue. The taste of her eclipsed the taste of every other woman. At last, he could sate himself in the pleasure of his angel, his sweet Rebekah.

She worked her hips sinuously against him, creating a searing heat in his groin that made him tremble with anticipation. His nostrils flared, filled with the scent of her feminine fragrance. He groaned again, breathing labored as her teeth nipped at his lower lip, and she caressed his face with gentle fingers.

He walked across the room, savoring the sensations of her mouth traveling over his heated flesh. When he eased her onto the bed against the pillows, one hand clung to his forearm. She was as reluctant as he to be separated.

"*Paciencia*," he told her softly, although she couldn't be any more impatient than he.

He undid his belt and removed his pants. Leaning his naked

body over her, he took in the vision she made. The wild tumble of hair, the sultry look in her dark brown eyes.

His hands, his mouth, and his tongue would reacquaint themselves with every inch of her delectable body. Not a single millimeter of silky brown skin would remain untouched.

Even if it took all night.

* * *

No LONGER HARNESSED by the restraint of propriety, Rebekah teetered on the edge of begging him to take her. She wanted his weight on her, pressing her down into the mattress, filling her body with his hard length. How could it be she'd lived without him for years, yet in a matter of weeks he'd become as vital to her as oxygen. Hunger thrummed in her veins, and only when her clothes joined his on the floor did she find she could breathe again.

Her breasts were heavy with desire, the nipples puckered and pointed, wanting the tug of his lips or the press of his broad chest—any part of him to touch or rub up against them to relieve the soreness.

His parted lips slipped over the soft mounds of her breasts with opened-mouthed kisses, the tip of his tongue grazing her nipples, intensifying the ache in her loins. His tongue danced over the hardened peaks before he finally enveloped one engorged nub into the warm, moist cavern of his mouth, offering the reprieve she so desperately craved. She arched her back in encouragement, sliding her hand across the smooth expanse of unyielding muscles in his back, moving her hips against him in urgent provocation.

His head dipped lower, licking the underside of her breasts, before his mouth moved down across her ribs. One hand trailed across her quivering stomach then traced the feminine curve of her waist and hips. She shuddered when his seeking fingers found the slick channel nestled below the dark triangle of curls between her thighs.

His stroking fingers primed her, dipping in and out of her until she imprinted her nails in the skin of his back.

"Oh...Rafe, I missed you, I missed you, I missed you," she whispered. "I need you now."

He ignored her plea and took his time.

He kissed her everywhere—between her legs, where she ached the most for him, down her thighs, her knees, her calves, and even her feet. When he finished, her body throbbed with sensory overload so acute she thought for sure she would lose her mind.

He rose up on his knees, and all she could do was lie there, looking at him through heavy-lidded eyes, her limp body drugged with passion and unable to move.

He grabbed her behind the knees and gently pulled her toward him. He spread her legs and positioned himself over her, pinning her wrists together above her head. The words he whispered in Spanish served to further inflame her.

The bulbous tip of his shaft probed the entrance to her body as he kissed her hungrily. Shifting his hips, he pushed forward to claim her, but he froze when he met with resistance.

"¿Que?" He frowned down at her, confusion in the gray depths of his eyes.

Now was not the time for explanations. Rebekah pressed the soles of her feet into the mattress and lifted her hips upward. She could accommodate him, and she didn't want him to hesitate.

"*Please,*" she panted.

He lowered his mouth to hers again, kissing her with such tenderness she felt choked with emotion. "*Mi amor,*" he groaned, tracing the curve of her hips with his fingers. "*T'eres tan bella... tan sexy.*" She arched her neck as he glided his mouth over her skin.

When he joined their bodies, she cried out from the raw charge of pleasure that coursed through her. It felt so good, too good, and she wanted more. She lifted her hips higher, countering his movements as he thrust into her body.

She closed her eyes against the tears of emotion threatening to overflow onto the sheets. The pain of the past slipped away as their panting breaths intermingled in between ravenous kisses. The connection between them was still as strong as ever, and she felt possessive, slipping her hands from his grasp so she could cling to him. He was hers, and as crazy as it seemed, she felt the need to protect him.

"Rebekah," he said, easing away from her. With his withdrawal, her eyes opened and a moan of protest slipped past her lips. "I want you from behind."

With the twist of his hands, he turned her onto her stomach and brought her to her knees. His lips pressed against the birthmark of light skin at the base of her spine. As he glided his palms over the smooth globes of her buttocks, she looked over her shoulder at him, looming big and powerful. Their eyes locked. He kneed her legs wider, and a sensuous shiver raced down her spine. Then he slid forward into her wet body. They fit together like reunited puzzle pieces, as if their bodies had been made for each other.

She trembled, desperate for the climax he dangled in front of her like a carrot. She curled her spine to take more of him, nearing the edge of what little control she had left as he continued, thrusting, thrusting. Reaching back, she hooked her arm around his powerful neck and parted her lips for his tongue.

* * *

RAFAEL FILLED her mouth the same way he filled her body. She was so responsive, so wet, and so tight. He swallowed the sweet little moans she made. No other man should have known the pleasure. He could hardly stomach the thought of her welcoming other men into her bed.

He pumped harder, faster, anger at himself and desire for her mixing into a volatile cocktail of emotions. With each advance of his hips, he aimed to obliterate the memory of every man who had come after him so all she remembered, all she wanted, all she needed, was him.

Rebekah's cries came faster and louder. Her hips pressed back against his with more urgency. He knew the moment she climaxed, her body trembling with a lack of control. He gritted his teeth, trying to hold on a little longer, but he was lost as her muscles contracted around him. The honeyed clamp of her body and her fervent cries of pleasure tore through the thin ribbon of his restraint. He gripped her hips and plunged himself deep, flames of ecstasy ripping through him. With a heavy groan, he soared into oblivion.

They collapsed into a pile on the mattress, his bones turned to mush, his large body slumped over her.

With effort, Rafael rolled onto his back. He had no doubt he'd been crushing her, but she hadn't moved or protested.

"Get under the covers," he said softly as he got up from the bed to turn out the light.

When he returned, he pulled Rebekah into his arms, cradling her close. It was a few moments before he was cognizant of the moisture on his shoulder.

"Rebekah?" He eased away, using the light that came through the large windows to get a look at her in the darkness. *Damnit.* He'd been too rough. She obviously hadn't had sex in awhile. "What's wrong? Did I hurt you?"

She shook her head, refusing to speak.

"*Dime, mi amor,*" he insisted. "Tell me what's wrong."

She kept her eyes closed. "Nothing," she whispered. "Except I love you so much."

His heart leapt at hearing the words he thought he'd never

hear her say again. New tears leaked from the corners of her eyes, and he kissed her lids then gathered her close, cradling the back of her head with his hand.

"Te amo también, mi amor," he said hoarsely against her temple. *"Demasiado."*

His jaw clenched into a hard line as he listened to her sniffles. He made a silent promise he would never, ever hurt her again. If she would give him the chance, he'd spend the rest of his life making up the past to her.

They fell asleep with their arms wrapped around each other and the comfortable weight of her head on his shoulder.

CHAPTER 14

*R*ebekah drifted awake, momentarily confused by the warmth of the body entangled with hers. She repositioned herself, feeling the slight ache of normally unused muscles. As she became aware of her surroundings, she remembered she lay in bed with Rafael.

She thought back over the years to all the times she'd lain awake, wondering where he was and who he was with, with nothing to fill her empty arms but the pillows beside her. Now, here she was with her first and only love, and before he'd drifted asleep, he'd said the same words he'd said years ago in the car on Stone Mountain: *I love you too much.*

With her eyes adjusted to the dark, Rebekah smiled to herself, trailing a finger down across his square jaw to his sensuous mouth. His lips twitched, but he didn't awaken, and she knew he probably wouldn't. He slept as soundly as a hibernating bear.

She smoothed her hand along his shoulder, over the image of Mixcoatl on his arm resting on the curve of her waist. When he groaned, she stilled her movements.

Was he having a bad dream?

He pulled her closer, which gave her a good idea of what he was dreaming about. His hardening flesh pressed against her thigh.

His eyes opened to unseeing slits before he came fully awake.

"*¿Estás bien?*" he asked sleepily.

"Yes, I'm fine." She rested a hand against his cheek. "I'm sorry I woke you."

"You didn't." He yawned, stretching. "Well, I guess you did. I was having an interesting dream, and then I woke up to this." He shifted his pelvis toward her.

Rebekah giggled. "That's not my fault." She ran her thumb over his lower lip. "What are we doing?" she asked quietly.

His face sobered. "I know what we're *not* doing," he said. At her questioning frown, he explained. "We're not just having sex. You said you love me, and I love you, and I've missed you. I've missed you every single day for the past nine years. We have a son, and I want us to try again, to see if we can make our marriage work. No other woman has ever made me feel this way, Rebekah. No other woman has ever come close."

His words thrilled her, but she still had doubts. "I'm scared," she admitted.

"I won't ever hurt and embarrass you again."

"Are you sure you can be satisfied…with one woman?"

"You always satisfied me," he said in a hard tone. "There was never anyone else when we were together."

Rebekah took a deep breath and let it out. "So we're calling off the lawyers?"

"First thing in the morning."

The thought of starting over filled Rebekah with joy and prompted her to kiss Rafael hard on the mouth. He hardened even more, and she laughingly pushed at his shoulders.

"No way," she teased. "I need sleep to rebuild my stamina. You're an athlete. I don't have the endurance you do."

"Maybe we can build up your stamina through exercise."

She wrinkled her nose. "Exercise?" she said with distaste.

"Mhmm. And you know what the best exercise is for building stamina?" Rafael asked. His forefinger ran down the side of her face.

"Running?"

"No."

"Jumping jacks?"

"No."

"Swimming?"

"No."

"What is it?" Rebekah asked in mock exasperation.

"Sex," Rafael answered with a grin.

"Wait a minute, you're going to build up my stamina for sex with sex?"

"Do you have a better idea?"

She inhaled sharply when his hand slid between her thighs. "No, I don't," she moaned.

He chuckled and nuzzled her neck.

"Rafe?"

"*Sí, mi ángel,*" he answered against her throat.

Rebekah stopped his hand before it drifted higher between her legs. She smiled into his eyes. "Lie back."

The urge to pleasure him, to show him how much she loved him, filled her. Feeling heady with power and excitement, she climbed on top of Rafael.

* * *

HE WATCHED her through lowered lids as she dropped little kisses on his chest. His excitement mounted as she slid lower over the plane of his stomach. When she took him in her mouth, his muscles tightened to hard, tense chords. Breathing became a

112

painful exercise. He mumbled something incoherent in Spanish even he didn't understand.

Her hair hung like a heavy curtain around her face as she worked her mouth and hands along his shaft, bringing him closer and closer to an orgasm. He warned her when he was about to come, but she continued undeterred, pulling, drawing every last bit of self-restraint until he could no longer withstand it. His control snapped. With a jerk, he went off like a bottle rocket, groaning, clenching the sheets, pumping his hips, and spilling into her mouth.

* * *

FEELING PLEASED WITH HERSELF, Rebekah crawled back up toward him, but she saw the question in his eyes.

"No," she said. "Only you."

He pulled her down to him and rolled her onto her back, fiercely devouring her lips. They kissed for a long time with Rebekah pinned beneath him. When he finally released her, she was breathless. He crushed her in a stronghold and pressed his lips against her temple.

"*Gracias.*"

She didn't know if he thanked her for what she'd just done or for never sharing such an intimate act with another man.

Perhaps it was both.

* * *

THE FOLLOWING MORNING, over a breakfast of coffee and *huevos rancheros*, Rebekah and Rafael discussed plans for the rest of the summer before his assistant arrived for work. They spoke to Rafael's attorney and left a message for Sterling Buchanan on the east coast. Once Lydia made her appearance, Rafael excused himself, but not before stealing a lingering kiss.

Over the course of the next two weeks, each day Rebekah and Ricardo explored different parts of the city, going to all the major tourist attractions and taking tours. Sometimes Rafael joined them. They visited the Kodak Theatre, the home of the Academy Awards every year. They took pictures at different spots on the Hollywood Walk of Fame, visited the courtyard of Grauman's Chinese theater off Hollywood Boulevard, and took a tour of the stars' homes.

They spent an entire day at Venice Beach, swimming, eating, and watching the street performers on the boardwalk, toured China Town, and spent a day at the Universal Studios theme park. In between, Rebekah managed to find time to get in some shopping too.

Despite the full days, at night, Rebekah had enough energy to accommodate the passion that consistently flared to life between her and Rafael. Because she had moved into his bedroom, Ricardo came in there regularly and climbed in between them to watch television. When he fell asleep, Rafael would carry him back to his room and he and Rebekah would spend the rest of the night talking or making love.

She was living a fairy tale, and the rekindled relationship between her and Rafael couldn't be better. But one night, the first doubts she'd had in weeks cropped up like ugly weeds in her field of happiness.

She awoke to an empty bed. Lifting her head, she saw Rafael standing in front of the windows. His head bent, he was looking at something in his hand. It appeared to be his phone.

"Rafe, honey?" He turned toward her, but with his back facing the windows, the shadows hid his face, and she couldn't see his expression. "Is something wrong?"

"No."

"Are you talking on the phone?"

A short pause. "No."

The clipped answer sent a trickle of unease down her spine. "What are you doing?"

He didn't answer right away, and his hesitation only heightened her feeling of disquiet. "I'm sending a text."

"At this hour?"

"It's nothing."

Rebekah swallowed. His unsatisfactory explanation did nothing to allay her fears. She wanted to probe further, but she was afraid of his answer. "If it's nothing, then come back to bed." She patted the empty space next to her where he should be.

He stood there for a moment, looking at her, and she hated she couldn't see his face—not even his eyes. Without another word, he turned off the phone and set it on top of the fireplace mantle. When he slipped into bed, she went immediately into his arms, seeking comfort from anxiety from an unknown source.

She stayed awake for a long time before sleep claimed her.

CHAPTER 15

*L*ess than a week later, Rebekah was a nervous wreck as she stood in front of the full-length mirror in the bedroom. Her fingers shook slightly as she slipped the Harry Winston long drop diamond earrings into her ears. She wished Rafael hadn't insisted on purchasing the expensive jewelry. Knowing they cost tens of thousands of dollars only made her more fretful about the evening. With her hair swept back into a stylish chignon, the prominent shimmer of the diamonds was on full display.

"You look beautiful." The stylist's encouraging smile appeared behind Rebekah in the full-length mirror. The younger woman smoothed her hands down the haute couture halter gown in printed silk organza. "How do you feel?"

Rebekah took a deep, calming breath and released it through her lipsticked lips. "Nervous."

"There's nothing to be nervous about. You look fabulous."

Easy for you to say.

She wouldn't be the one walking the red carpet at Grauman's Chinese Theatre tonight. With butterflies running rampant in her stomach, Rebekah took another deep breath and assessed her reflection.

She had to admit, the pastel colors were flattering against her dark skin, and since Rafael liked her in lighter colors, she knew he'd appreciate what he saw. The full, flowing skirt of the dress draped along the carpet and made her feel elegant and stylish.

She and Rafael were on their way to the movie premiere of Dwayne "The Rock" Johnson's latest action flick. When Rafael started wrestling for the WWE, Dwayne had advised him on how to control his wrestling image, based on his own years of experience in the business. Even after Dwayne left wrestling for Hollywood, he and Rafael had remained friends.

"This one is my favorite," Rebekah said with finality.

Thanks to a few phone calls from Lydia, since yesterday afternoon, dresses, undergarments, and shoes had been arriving at the house. Of all the dresses she'd received, Rebekah liked this one the best for comfort and style.

"We should see what Mr. Lopez thinks."

Rebekah nodded her agreement, and after one last look at her reflection, she followed the stylist out the door to the living room.

"...now is not a good time," Rafael was saying as they entered.

His eyebrows were drawn together in an angry frown, and the white-knuckled grip on his cell phone was so tight she wouldn't have been surprised if it shattered in his grasp. When he noted their entrance, his face lightened immediately.

"I have to go. I'll call you later," he said in a curt tone.

Rebekah studied his features. Dressed in a classic tuxedo and bow tie, he epitomized raw sex appeal, but she noted the tension around his mouth and the emotion swirling in his eyes.

"Who was that?" she asked.

"Nothing for you to worry about," he said with a crooked smile.

Normally, his smile would have her swooning, but it didn't work this time because she knew something was amiss, and he was keeping it from her.

He took her hand and prompted her into a slow twirl. "Is this the one you've decided on?" he asked, his voice filled with male appreciation.

He purposely changed the subject, and she allowed him to—for now. She didn't want to spoil the evening, but she intended to question him further at a later time.

"Yes. How do I look?" She placed one hand on her hip and posed sideways for him.

"*Caliente.*"

"I'm serious."

"So am I. You're going to steal the show."

"Now for the shoes, and you'll be ready to go," the stylist interjected, sounding pleased.

Minutes later, they stood at the front door, saying their goodbyes to Ricardo, with promises to have The Rock's autograph with them upon their return. He did his happy dance and then hurried off to his room.

In the back of the hired limo, Rebekah threaded her fingers through Rafael's and rested her head on his shoulder as she listened to the instructions from his male publicist. She marveled at how much Rafael's life had changed, and she recognized the loyalty and professionalism of everyone he employed. They supported him and made him look good.

When he had asked her to attend the premiere with him, her initial thought was to decline. Then she remembered all the wrestling bouts she'd missed in the early years of their marriage, and she changed her mind. Although this wasn't his event, he wanted her by his side, and she would support him.

When they pulled up outside Grauman's Chinese Theatre,

an intimidating crowd of thousands waited for the arrival of the celebrities. Her stomach tangled into knots, but she forced herself to calm down. Rafael gave her hand a reassuring squeeze before he slipped from the vehicle. She and his publicist followed soon after but hung back out of the line of the cameras while he posed for photographers. Some yelled out his name, some called him by his wrestling name, *La Sombra*. Others yelled out questions, which he didn't answer, only smiled.

He answered questions posed by a couple of the celebrity entertainment correspondents who interviewed him for a few minutes each. He then walked up to the barricade where the onlookers stood, signed a few autographs, and shook hands with the excited fans. As he stepped back onto the red carpet, the publicist prodded Rebekah forward. Rafael reached for her hand, making sure to use his body to protect her from the cameras. That didn't stop the photographers from their rapid-fire camera snapping and from hurtling questions at them.

"Rafael, Rafael, who's the lovely lady?"

"Is she the future Mrs. Lopez?"

"Is your lady friend an actress? What's her name?"

Without stopping or answering questions, they entered the theatre.

* * *

"RICKY, TIME FOR LUNCH, SWEETIE," Rebekah called from the kitchen.

Rafael and Lydia had gone to a ribbon-cutting ceremony for one of the new gyms that was opening. She and Ricardo were the only ones at the house since she sent the housekeeper home with pay for the day. Just as she set the two plates of food on the table by the window, the telephone rang. She recognized the number as her brother's.

"Hi, Adam."

"Bekah, it's me!" Her sister's excited voice came through on the line.

"Samirah? What are you doing back in the country?"

"When did you last check your email?" her sister countered. "I sent you guys a message letting you know I'd be back for a couple of weeks. I just got in yesterday, and I'm staying at Adam's."

"I know you're going up to Atlanta to see Mom and Dad, right?"

"*Of course.* I'll spend a few days there before I leave the country again." Her younger sister could never stay put for too long. She spoke several languages fluently and flitted around the world from one exciting locale to another. "What are you up to?"

"I just made lunch for me and Ricky—ham and cheese in corn tortillas."

"*Sincronizadas?* Oh, man, I love those things. The best ones I ever had were at this little roadside shack in Chiapas. Ooh, I can still taste them."

"Yeah, well, whatever they're called, Ricky and I are hooked on them, thanks to Rafael's housekeeper." She walked toward the bedroom. "Ricky, lunch is ready."

"Coming, Mom."

Rebekah headed back toward the kitchen. "Samirah, you really need to stop eating just anywhere. You're going to get sick one of these days."

"I have a cast iron stomach," her sister said. "Anyway, how else do you expect me to get the true experience of a culture if I don't eat what the locals eat?"

Rebekah sighed. "I just want you to be careful. I don't know where you got this sense of adventure from."

Samirah laughed. "I don't either, but I guess someone has to have some fun in the family. Adam's a square and you're Miss Goody-Goody. Have you earned your halo and wings yet?"

Rebekah picked up one of the toasted corn tortillas filled with ham and oozing with cheese. "Is that why you called—to give me a hard time?" she asked before taking a bite. She sat in a chair at the table.

"No. I called because I wanted to ask you what you're doing inside *People* magazine."

"*What?*"

"You heard me. Don't tell me you didn't know?"

"No, I didn't know!"

Samirah laughed. "Well, you're going to love this—seeing as how you like being in the spotlight." Rebekah groaned. "Don't worry, it's not bad. You look amazing in that dress, by the way. So, I'm standing in line at the grocery store—because our dear brother has already put me to work because he's letting me crash at his place for free—and I pick up the latest issue of *People*. I'm flipping through the magazine, and the next thing I know, I see a picture of you and Rafe. He's holding your hand, and you're just a step or two behind him. The caption reads, 'Who's the mystery woman with Rafael Lopez?' You're famous!"

Samirah's exuberance was not catching. "I don't want to be famous."

"Well, it's out of your hands now. Your photo's in the magazine for millions of people to see. I bought a copy. Would you autograph mine for me?"

"I'm going to choke you the next time I see you."

"Tsk, tsk, not very sisterly of you," Samirah joked. "What's going on with you and Rafe? Are you two officially back together?"

"Well..."

Samirah screamed so loud, Rebekah had to pull the phone away from her ear. "You are!"

"We're still working on it, okay? We're starting over...dating. It's been a long time, so we're getting to know each other again."

"Aw. That's so cute. Like Romeo and Juliet."

"Romeo and Juliet died."

"Oh yeah."

Ricardo came into the room and picked up his plate and juice. "Can I eat in my room?" he asked in a loud whisper.

Rebekah nodded. "Don't make a mess," she mouthed to him before he nodded and walked away.

"Name a romantic couple who lived happily ever after."

"Samirah, did you hear what I said? We're still working it out."

"Are you working it out in the bedroom too?"

"Samirah!"

"Okay, okay, I'll leave it alone, but I know that's a yes." Rebekah smiled faintly and shook her head. "I just remember how sad you were after the break up. It was really hard to watch."

"I know. I wasn't myself for awhile."

In a quiet voice, Samirah asked, "So you've forgiven him?"

"It was a long time ago, and he's trying really hard. He still says nothing happened that night, and...I believe him. I really love him, Samirah, and I think we can work this out. We both want to."

She hadn't yet spoken to Rafael about the middle of the night text and the phone call the day of the movie premiere a few days ago. She had delayed asking him about it long enough. She resolved to get answers when he came home.

"Oh, Bekah, I'm so excited for you. Do what makes you happy." She could hear the catch in her sister's voice. "I hope I find my Prince Charming one day."

"You have to stay in one place long enough to do that."

"Forget it. I've got at least a few more years of travel left in me. After I leave Miami, I'm off to Morocco."

"See what I mean?"

"Hey, what about that guy you were dating—Carl...Carl...?"

"Carlton. What about him?"

"What happened to him?"

"He and I stopped seeing each other once I found out Rafe and I were still married. I spoke to him about a week ago and explained we're working on our marriage. He wasn't happy about it."

"I never met Carlton. What was he like?"

The intercom buzzed. "Hold on, Samirah. Someone's at the gate, and I'm expecting a package for Rafe."

"No, I'll call you later when we have more time to chat. I need to make another phone call. Tell my brother-in-law he better not hurt you again, or he'll have to deal with me."

"I will. Bye, hon."

Rebekah buzzed the deliveryman in the gate. She signed for the package and was on her way to drop it off in the bedroom when the doorbell rang.

Did he forget something?

She swung open the door, but it wasn't the deliveryman. A woman stood on the other side. Right away, Rebekah noted the stylish sunglasses on the woman's head, which kept her long dark hair out of her face, the expensive handbag, and flattering sundress.

"Yes?" She must have slipped in behind the courier, which by itself was cause for alarm. She didn't look like a crazed fan, but judging a book by its cover was always a bad idea.

"Who are you?" the woman asked. Her eyes narrowed. "You're in *People* magazine. Are you the wife?" A frown of irritation marred her forehead.

"Who are you?" Rebekah demanded.

"Is Rafe here?" She tried to peer around Rebekah.

Rebekah didn't like the familiar manner in which the other woman said her husband's name. Then she had the audacity to try to brush past Rebekah, but she put up her hand to stop her from entering. The woman's chest collided with Rebekah's palm.

"Excuse me, who are you?" she asked again in a firmer voice. Whoever this woman was, she obviously didn't know her place.

The other woman's face became a flushed, angry scowl. "I'm Cynthia," she said, holding up her left hand to show a diamond solitaire. "Didn't Rafe tell you? I'm his fiancée."

CHAPTER 16

*R*ebekah sat on the edge of the bed with her fingers curled into the mattress. Stunned didn't adequately describe what she felt. Flabbergasted and dumbfounded better explained her state of mind. Cynthia had provided a lot of information about her relationship with Rafael before she left.

She could hear him coming down the hall. *Humming.* As if everything was just fine. She wouldn't cry. She would give him a chance to explain, because there had to be a perfectly reasonable explanation.

A few steps into the room, he stopped short when he saw her glaring at him. The dimples disappeared from his smiling face.

"What's wrong, *mi amor?*"

Rebekah hardened her heart against the words of affection. "Who is Cynthia?"

When the color drained from his face, she got her answer. Her blood ran cold. "You *bastard!*" she screamed. She hopped to her feet and grabbed the nearest object—a pillow—and tossed it across the room at him.

He deflected it with ease. "Wait a minute. I can explain."

"Explain? Explain this, you—you—" Rebekah pulled open

the top drawer of the nightstand and started tossing objects at him—pens, a notepad, batteries. "'No other woman has ever come close,'" she said, mimicking his words from several weeks ago. "Do you remember that—*liar!*"

"I never lied to you," Rafael said, dodging an iPod and the connected ear buds. "Let's talk."

"There's nothing to talk about." She tossed one of her shoes at him. "The time for talking is over, and I don't want to hear any more lies. How long did you think you could continue to have sex with both of us at the same time?"

"That never happened."

"That's not what she said. Two women for Rafe. Just like old times, wasn't it?"

"Stop it, Rebekah."

"Stupid, naive Rebekah. You probably couldn't believe your luck. You'd fooled me again. You'd convinced me I was the most important thing in your life, the only woman you wanted, when at the same time you had your fiancée visiting from New York."

"She had no right to come here and say what she did. I broke things off with her a long time ago."

"Really? Did you tell *her* it's over, because when she came here, she had a different story to tell. Oh, wait, am I the other woman in this scenario?"

"Enough! Everything you're saying is incorrect." He made a movement toward her, and she tossed the other shoe in her hand at him. It stopped him for second, bouncing off his chest and landing on the floor.

She made a mad dash to scramble across the bed.

"Oh no, you don't." Rafael grabbed onto her ankles and eased her backward across the mattress before she could make it to the other side. The hem of her dress rode up her thighs.

Rebekah tried to kick at him, but he held her tight and flipped her over onto her back. "You're going to listen to me whether you want to or not."

To her chagrin, when she swung at him, he blocked the blow with his forearm. She grimaced, cradling her arm against her chest.

"*Maldito sea*! When the hell did you get so violent?" he growled.

"Get up!"

"No." He pinned her arms to the bed with one hand. Rebekah wiggled angrily, but he didn't budge. "I can stay here all day," he said calmly.

Finally, she halted her movements. Her breath came in short, angry spurts. She knew she could wear herself out if she didn't stop because she couldn't match his strength. Refusing to look at him, she stared up at the ceiling.

"Will you let me explain?"

Rebekah lowered her lids. She wouldn't cry. *Wouldn't*. But the pain was so acute, tearing through her with the precision of a blade.

"How could you?" she whispered brokenly. "You're engaged —about to marry another woman—when I haven't even...I've never...been with anyone but you."

His hold on her loosened, and she opened her eyes to see the look of shock on his face. "No one?"

She pushed him away and sat up.

She hadn't meant to admit that, but in her emotional state, the words flew past her lips before she could stop them. "After we split, I was hurting, and I didn't want to be with anyone until we got a divorce." She shrugged. "I definitely didn't want to get involved with anyone when I found out I was pregnant. When Ricky was born, I got busy with work, going to school full-time, and being a mother." She pressed her lips together, thinking about how she'd relied on these excuses over the years so she wouldn't have to deal with the pathetic truth—that she hadn't wanted to sleep with anyone else. No other man had ever come close to making her feel the way he did. "By the time I started dating, I was back at my father's church regularly and had pretty much decided I would go back to the way I was raised, and I would only date *nice* men."

They sat in silence for awhile, and then Rafael ran a weary hand over his face. "She was never my fiancée. We had a few dates, and that was it. There was something a little off about her, so I ended it right away."

"Then why were you texting her in the middle of the night? And don't try to deny it, because I know it was her. Why didn't you tell me about her?"

"Because…"

"Why?" she screamed at him.

"Because I didn't want to lose you!" he yelled back. He bolted from the bed. Standing with his back to her, he shoved his hands into pockets, his body still as a statue. "The first time I lost you, it ripped my heart out. I didn't want you to find out about her because I know how you feel about living your life in the public eye. I was trying to fix the situation before you found out.

"Cynthia lives in New York, and our very short—I guess you could call it an acquaintance—had been long distance from the beginning. When I met her, I'd been retired for a year already and had a lot of time on my hands. Too much time. I started thinking about having children, but after a few dates, I realized I'd made a mistake. She became obsessed with everything about me. It was odd. Then she constantly asked me about money and couldn't stop talking about how her status would change if we got married. I never even suggested marriage to her."

He faced her again. "As a public figure, you never know who wants to be close to you for you or for your celebrity status and your money. With Cynthia, I thought maybe I'd finally found someone who didn't care."

"How did it end?" Rebekah asked quietly.

"I told her she was a great person but it wasn't working out.

Awhile back, she asked me for money, and I refused to give it to her. She became hysterical. She wanted to know how I could be so cold after everything we'd been to each other." He shook his head. "I was on my way to New York to see her—to try to talk some sense into her in person—when I stopped in Atlanta to visit you. When I got to New York, I told her I had a son and I was still married, thinking maybe she would give up. It worked for awhile, but then she started again. She threatened to spread negative rumors about me to the media. I think she's unbalanced. Lydia's getting me a new phone number and my attorney drafted a complaint to the police, but it seems I'll have to take more drastic measures. For her to show up here today and claim to be my fiancée..." He shook his head. "I may have to take legal action against her."

"She had a ring."

"I *never* gave her a ring. I don't want to have anything to do with her."

Rebekah wrapped her arms around her torso and walked over to stare into the fireplace. Were there other women from his past who would surface?

Just as she'd feared, his life in the spotlight was problematic. Her heart ached for what she was about to lose. There would be no more late nights curled up in bed listening to him explain the preparation and behind-the-scenes events of his matches as they watched them on video. She would no longer be awakened in the middle of the night by Rafael's kisses and the urgent caress of his hands across her skin. No more trips to the beach to build sand castles, no more watching her son grow into a young man with the help of his father, and no more stroking her fingers across the silky hairs of Rafael's head until he fell asleep.

She blinked back the tears and faced him. "She came to our —your house, Rafe. I don't know if I can handle all these women all the time. When does it stop?"

"You're the only woman in my life and the only one who's ever mattered to me. There are no other women."

"There will always be other women." Her thoughts were like heavy sandbags, weighing down her hopes and dreams.

Rafael took a deep breath. "I can't control what they do, Rebekah. I can only control the actions of Rafael Lopez." His eyes blazed with the urgency of his explanation. "I intend to hold you in my arms every night and wake up next to you every morning. I'll do my best to provide for you and Ricardo. But there is one thing I won't do. I won't—*can't* go back to living without you and my son."

"If I leave—"

"I'll follow you."

She paused. "You can't. Your life is here."

"My life is with you, and your life is with me. That's the way it was nine years ago, and that's the way it is now." There was a hard, determined set to his jaw and an embattled, fierce gleam in his eye. "I won't accept a lifelong punishment for a mistake in judgment I made almost ten years ago, and I won't be punished for someone else's actions."

"We agreed to try for awhile, but it's obvious this isn't going to work."

"Obvious to you, maybe, but not to me." He came slowly toward her. Tension uncoiled in her body as he drew nearer. "I've told you she means nothing to me, and she had no right to come here because our relationship has been over for a year now."

"It's not just about *her*."

"Then what is it about?" Rafael demanded.

"It's about *all of them*," Rebekah answered. "The groupies, for one. And I've seen pictures of some of the women you dated in the past. How am I supposed to compete against them—models, actresses? They're beautiful and well-dressed and–and fabulous. I'm a science teacher!"

His face softened. "There's no competition between you and anyone else. I meant what I said before. No one else has ever come close."

The sincerity in his voice overwhelmed her. She so desperately needed to believe those words. "Never?"

"Never." He extended his hand to her, and she rested hers in it. "And you are the sexiest science teacher alive."

She gave him a tentative smile. "They don't give out awards for that."

He smiled back. "They should. If they did, you'd take the title every year."

Rebekah shook her head. "You always know what to say, Rafe. No wonder you were able to steal me away from family." She looked into his eyes. "No more secrets. We're in this together."

"Are you sure you can handle it?"

Rebekah nodded. "I can handle it, no matter what comes our way."

"Bad press? Rumors?"

Rebekah nodded.

He quirked an eyebrow. "No more overreacting? You'll listen first before you start throwing things?"

She glanced at the items strewn across the carpet. With an embarrassed smile, she said, "No more overreacting. I'll listen first." She wrapped her arms around his wide torso and gazed up at him. "I have a teeny-weeny jealous streak."

"Me too." Rafael pressed a quick kiss to her forehead. "Let me show you something." He pulled out his wallet and lifted a wrinkled old photograph from it. "I couldn't make myself get rid of it."

It was a ten-year-old photo of the two of them. She hadn't wanted him to take the photo that day because she'd wanted to fix her hair first, but he'd insisted she was beautiful and convinced her cornrows were fine. Their cheeks were pressed together, and she'd hammed it up by puckering her lips toward the camera in a saucy pose.

Her eyes filled with tears. "I can't believe you still have that silly picture." She had a duplicate copy in a box filled with mementos and photos of them at the top of her closet in her Atlanta home.

"I want us to be like that again."

She swallowed past the lump in her throat. "I do too."

Rafael got down on one knee in front of her. "I made a stop on the way home today." He lifted a velvet-covered black box from his slacks and opened it to reveal a large, emerald cut diamond ring with a platinum band. "I planned to take you to dinner and give this to you."

"Oh my goodness," Rebekah breathed. It was a far cry from the gold wedding band she still had tucked in the same box in her closet.

"I couldn't afford to get you an engagement ring the first time," Rafael began, his eyes filled with love and adoration. "If you'll let me, I'll spend the rest of my life giving you everything you deserve. Rebekah, will you marry me—again?"

The image of him blurred behind a screen of tears that overflowed onto her cheeks. She nodded vigorously. "Yes. I'll marry you," she said. "As many times as you like."

He slipped the ring on her trembling finger, and they sealed the promise with a kiss.

EPILOGUE

*T*he rented house in Maui couldn't have been a better choice for a first honeymoon. It was right on the beach, and as long as they kept the doors to the balcony slightly ajar as they had them right now, they could listen to the sound of the ocean only feet away.

"It's nice having an assistant," Rebekah said idly.

Lydia had handled the reservations for their travel, and the entire trip had gone smoothly. She and Rafael had been in Hawaii for two days while Ricardo remained in California with the temporary nanny they'd hired for the two weeks they would be gone. They'd waited until he was acclimated to his new school before taking the trip.

Rebekah lay on top of Rafael, her head nestled against his shoulder. The only thing covering their naked bodies was his shirt draped across her hips. The arm along her bare back held her close, and Rebekah stroked his head, running her fingers through the silky short hairs in a comforting motion. Their original intention of going sightseeing got postponed in favor of an afternoon of making love.

"I've been wondering about something for weeks. What did my father say to you at the wedding?"

The outdoor ceremony had taken place at the home of one of Rafael's friends. A small, intimate affair, only close friends and family attended the renewing of their vows.

"He threatened to hurt me if I ever messed up again. Then he welcomed me into the family."

Rebekah smiled and placed a gentle kiss on the strong, dark column of his throat. "At least you received the welcome you've always wanted."

"It wasn't quite what I had hoped for, but I can live with it. Samirah and your brother also threatened me."

"You'd better behave yourself then. What about my mother?"

"No, your mother didn't say anything. She's a good woman. I've always liked her. Much nicer than her husband." The last sentence sounded slurred.

Rebekah glanced at him. His eyes were closed. "What are you doing? Don't you dare go to sleep on me."

"Then stop stroking my hair."

When she stopped, he took her hand and replaced it on his head.

Rebekah continued to caress his head. "Tell me you love me," she said softly.

"*Te amo.*"

"How much?" She already knew the answer, but it never failed to make her glow whenever he said it.

"*Demasiado.*"

She continued to caress his head until her fingers slowed. She drifted into contented slumber with him, lulled to sleep by the sound of the waves rolling up to drag sand into the sea.

ALSO BY DELANEY DIAMOND

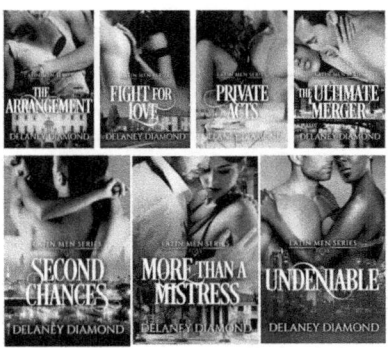

Check out the entire Latin Men series with heroes from Mexico, Ecuador, Brazil, and Argentina: The Arrangement, Fight for Love, Private Acts, The Ultimate Merger, Second Chances, More Than a Mistress, and Undeniable.

ABOUT THE AUTHOR

Delaney Diamond is the USA Today Bestselling Author of sweet, sensual, passionate romance novels. Originally from the U.S. Virgin Islands, she now lives in Atlanta, Georgia. She reads romance novels, mysteries, thrillers, and a fair amount of nonfiction. When she's not busy reading or writing, she's in the kitchen trying out new recipes, dining at one of her favorite restaurants, or traveling to an interesting locale.

Enjoy free reads on her website. Join her mailing list to get sneak peeks, notices of sale prices, and find out about new releases.

Join her mailing list
www.delaneydiamond.com

facebook.com/DelaneyDiamond
twitter.com/DelaneyDiamond
bookbub.com/authors/delaney-diamond
pinterest.com/delaneydiamond

www.ingramcontent.com/pod-product-compliance
Lightning Source LLC
Chambersburg PA
CBHW051252170626
46809CB00004B/1615